Cox

THE
SEAGULL
LIBRARY OF
GERMAN
LITERATURE

Cox

or, The Course of Time

CHRISTOPH RANSMAYR

Translated by Simon Pare

LONDON NEW YORK CALCUTTA

This publication has been supported by a grant from
the Goethe-Institut India

Seagull Books, 2022

Originally published in German as *Cox oder Der Lauf der Zeit*
© S. Fischer Verlag GmbH, Frankfurt am Main, 2016

First published in English translation by Seagull Books, 2020
English translation © Simon Pare, 2020

Published as part of the Seagull Library of German Literature, 2022

The translator would like to thank the Kunststiftung Nordrhein-
Westfalen and the Europäisches Übersetzer-Kollegium in Straelen for
the Atriumsgespräch workshop with Christoph Ransmayr and his
translators in June 2017.

ISBN 978 1 8030 9 040 5

British Library Cataloguing-in-Publication Data
A catalogue record for this book is available from the British Library.

Typeset by Seagull Books, Calcutta, India
Printed and bound by WordsWorth India, New Delhi, India

To Ān

Contents

Arrival

Cox reached the Chinese mainland under slack sails on the morning of the October day on which Qiánlóng, the most powerful man in the world and Emperor of China, had the noses of twenty-seven tax collectors and bond dealers cut off.

On that mild autumn day, banks of mist drifted over the unruffled waters of the Qiántáng whose sandy bed, melting into multiple side channels, had been dredged by more than two hundred thousand forced labourers using shovels and baskets so that, in accordance with the Emperor's wishes, an error of nature might be corrected and the now-navigable river might link the sea and Hángzhōu Bay with the city.

1

Again and again, the shifting fog hid the incoming ship from the eyes of the crowd gathered at the execution site by the harbour's edge. According to police reports, two thousand one hundred spectators, witnesses to Emperor Qiánlóng's infallibility and righteousness, many of them in their finest clothing, were waiting for the executioner to appear, chatting or standing in solemn silence as they watched the three-masted barquentine float towards them through the river mist, repeatedly fading from view and exuding greater menace with every reappearance. What a ship!

Even some of the condemned men chained to their stakes raised their heads to gaze at the silently drifting barquentine with its deep-blue square and fore-and-aft rig, while those assembled around the scaffold seemed to have forgotten that all the world's attention was solely beholden to the Emperor and to the execution of his will, to none but the Son of Heaven who condescended only out of benevolence to share people's affection and gazes with other humans and creatures.

No flood, no volcanic eruption and no earth tremor, not even an eclipse of the sun, could warrant that even a single thought should turn away without permission from the Emperor's glory and omnipotence to the events of the everyday world.

The Emperor had demonstrated with the deepening of the Qiántáng that his will could transport an entire city to the sea, and bring the sea to the gardens and parks of Hángzhōu. Ever since, the swelling tide had borne approaching ships to the city's quays and warehouses like offerings from the ocean, while the river, reversing its flow to the alternating rhythm of low and high tide, could float entire fleets as a mirror of imperial might.

But what did His Imperial Majesty matter, whose laws determined every twitch of life, the course of the river, the coastlines, the glances people exchanged and their inner-most thoughts, now that an unfamiliar tall ship came gliding over the black waters of the Qiántáng, stinking of lime from the tanneries? The Emperor was invisible. The ship, on the other hand, was not—or was hidden from view for only a few heartbeats before the banks of mist once more released it into unambiguous reality.

Resting in their litters or under canopies among the crowd gathered at the place of execution, some mandarins had begun to mutter among themselves about recent rumours —whisperings in the court's many shadowy corners of the arrival of an English sailing ship laden with precious automata and timepieces. But the whisperers never pointed at the barquentine, glancing around anxiously after every sentence to check that none of the Emperor's many ears were listening or that none of his many eyes were noting them, subjects clad in embroidered cloaks or fur-trimmed robes, their names easily ascertained by a policeman or a secret agent, harbouring forbidden doubts about His Holy Highness's plans for that morning; naturally, the condemned stood where they were standing because His Radiant Highness had willed it so. Yet was it really *His* will that this enormous, blue-rigged ship should be holding a course towards one of the most magnificent and prosperous cities in the empire?

Qiánlóng, whether invisible or shimmering in red-gold and silk, was omnipresent; a god. Although he was ending his inspection tour of seven provinces in Hángzhou, and would return to Běijīng with his retinue of over five thousand courtiers on board a fleet of thirty-five ships via the Grand Canal—a waterway dug for his personal use—none of the city's inhabitants, not one of its most senior officials, had so much as glimpsed him during his visit. After all, the Emperor did not need to tire his eyes with the sight of everyday nuisances, nor his voice with conversation or speeches. Everything there was to see or to say, his subjects said or saw for him; and he—he saw everything, even through closed eyes, and heard everything, even while asleep.

Guarded by hundreds of armoured warriors, Qiánlóng, Son of Heaven and Lord of Time, was floating that morning in feverish dreams high above the towers and roofs of Hángzhōu; high above the drifting fog, somewhere among dark-green hills where the autumn air was redolent with mild aromas, and the empire's finest tea was plucked; he lay there like a babe, in a bed suspended from the red-lacquered beams of his splendid tent by four silken tresses interwoven with purple threads and perfumed with oils of lavender and violet. Now and then, nightingale feathers stitched to its gossamer curtains fluttered sluggishly in the draught.

Spurning the luxury of the palaces of Hángzhōu, which for weeks had stood ready but empty, the court had pitched its tents and His Holy Highness's silk marquee high above the city, because the travelling Emperor sometimes preferred the wind and the transience of a fortress of canvas, guy-lines and pennants to apartments and walls liable to conceal hidden dangers or prove to be traps set by conspirators and assassins. From the hilltops, though, it looked as if Qiánlóng were laying siege to one of his own cities.

Surrounded by a sea of papers, solicitations, verdicts, calligraphy and poetry, expert reports and watercolours, and countless documents still bound and sealed that he was intending to read and inspect, approve, admire or reject that day, as he did in the early hours of every other day, he lay ensnared in racing dreams from which he woke with a start when his senior valet sought to protect a valuable deed from the feverish ruler's cramps and dry his perspiring brow with a piece of cambric sprinkled with lotus essence.

No! *No*! *Get out*! Qiánlóng, a forty-two-year-old man who looked almost delicate amid the splendour of his cushions and bedclothes, turned away like an irate child. He wanted everything, even the jumble of rustling papers among which he tossed and turned, to be left exactly where and how it was. A barely perceptible suggestion of a wagging index finger had sufficed to send the servant's hands darting back into frozen readiness.

Yet which of the silently bowing servants and physicians in attendance, all of them forbidden on pain of death to breathe a word outside this tent about His Holy Highness's fever or other possible ailments, and which of the soldiers of the imperial guard, still as stone in their crimson armour as they encircled the tent like one motionless, breathing carapace, would have dared to doubt that the Emperor, though he lay sweat-soaked and fever-ridden in his floating bed, was not also at this moment—simultaneously!—down below, present in the mist-cloaked city, even present among the twenty-seven swindlers awaiting mutilation. Present too in the black waters of the harbour, in which an English barquentine was now running out the anchor chains with a clatter.

As if this crowd-silencing clatter were his cue to appear, and even before the anchor had hit the bottom and the chains had tautened, a scrawny man with a waist-length plait stepped wordlessly towards the first of the twenty-seven stakes: the executioner. He bowed curtly to the condemned man who began to whimper with fear, then used his left thumb to force up the tip of the man's nose before placing a scimitar against its underside and, with a jerk, sliced up through the nasal bone to just below the man's forehead.

The ensuing shriek of pain, which began with a spurt of blood from a strangely empty and suddenly skull-like face, and rose in time to the executioner's progress from stake to stake where he bowed and made identical incisions, grew into a deafening howl, mingling here and there with first stifled, then swelling bursts of laughter. Now, after losing face, these greedy pigs were losing their noses too! And this was a mild punishment—too mild a punishment—for having sold worthless bonds at the stock exchanges of Běijīng and Shànghai and Hángzhōu, and trying to cover up the scam with tax revenues—the Emperor's gold! They should grovel gratefully before their judges, for, in the opinion of some of those guffawing at the foot of the scaffold, they should also have had their dicks cut off and stuffed up their arses until shit backed up into their mouths. It was an act of mercy that blood spouted only from these bastards' flattened faces, that only their noses went bouncing across the boards of the scaffold like fallen fruit!

Two shaggy dogs, following closely on the executioner's heels, sniffed at the skipping spoils but did not touch them. That was the task of a horde of crows which swooped down from the roofs of a bell-shaped pagoda a few screams and breaths before the final prisoner lost his nose, eventually shunning, for inexplicable reasons, only four or five noses which they left lying there amid a maze of bloody stains. Did the Emperor, wherever he might be in his invisibility, share the feelings of the laughing witnesses to his justice, and smile?

As if the rattle of the anchor chains and the subsequent screams of pain issuing from the city far below had finally released him from his tangled dreams, high up among the mountain chains the Son of Heaven sat up in his sickbed which was still rocking gently under the impetus of his latest cramps. However, not even the valet kneeling beside this swaying bed understood Qiánlóng's mumbled words: So has he arrived? Has the Englishman arrived?

Alister Cox, a clockmaker and automaton-builder from London, and master of over nine hundred fine mechanics, jewellers and gold- and silversmiths, stood at the rail of the three-masted *Sirius* and shivered despite the morning sun that had already climbed high above the hills of

Hángzhōu and was burning off the mist hanging over the black water.

Cold. Cold. *Damn.*

During the storm-ravaged seven-month voyage from Southampton along the malaria-ridden African coast, around the Cape of Good Hope and via the malaria-ridden ports of India and South-East Asia to this stinking Hángzhōu Bay, the *Sirius* had been his sole, long-detested dwelling place and refuge. The ship had suffered two broken masts on the journey and both times—first off the coast of Senegal, then in the crazed currents around Sumatra—been in danger of foundering, along with its precious cargo.

Yet, as if protected by an almighty hand, a Noah's Ark filled with wondrous metal creatures—jewel-encrusted silver and gold peacocks fanning their tails, mechanical leopards, monkeys and silver-furred Arctic foxes, kingfishers, nightingales and chameleons made of gilded copper whose colour could change from ruby red to emerald green—the *Sirius* had not gone to the bottom but, following long repairs on hostile shores, hoisted its sails once more and set course for a land of promise ruled by a divine emperor.

In the stormy nights during which even the captain gave up believing that his ship could withstand the crashing waves, Cox, who had never been to sea before, had developed a curious symptom with which he reacted to every subsequent awe-inspiring event or threat: at the first sign of danger, even in the tropical heat of South-East Asia or Indonesia, he began to shiver. Those around him would occasionally hear his teeth chatter. And his chill this particular sunny morning was caused by a glance through the beautifully engraved telescope he intended to present to the Emperor of China at his first audience.

The crew of the *Sirius*, and Cox too, had interpreted the laughter, shouting and booming gongs, borne by a rising breeze across the calm waters to the *Sirius*'s worm-eaten gunwales, as sounds of celebration. The Chinese Emperor had ordered celebrations for the arrival of the Western world's most gifted automaton-builder and clockmaker! And indeed, into the sky shot rockets of such dazzling intensity that their rainbow-coloured trails of smoke, winding their way in hurtling spirals towards the zenith in the wake of bright explosions, did not pale in the sunlight. Yet Cox's view through the telescope revealed not a flower-bedecked bandstand or flagpoles but, rather, twenty-seven stakes on a scaffold—proof that this was no celebration.

Cox shivered. He saw before him, once more, the imperial emissaries, two men with long plaits, dressed in clothes curiously plain-cut yet made of silk and shimmering wool, who had delivered the invitation from the Emperor of

China during that disastrous autumn two years ago when his daughter Abigail—his sun, his star, a child of five—had died from whooping cough.

Since Cox had refused to interrupt his wake and greet the noble visitors in the reception room, the emissaries had approached Abigail's bier. He hadn't eaten for three days, had hardly drunk anything either, and he heard the East India Company interpreter's translation of the envoys' words as if from afar:

Master Alister Cox was requested in the name of the Son of Heaven and august Emperor Qiánlóng to come to the court in Běijīng as the first Westerner ever to take up quarters in a Forbidden City, and create unprecedented works according to the plans and dreams of His Holy Highness, the greatest and most passionate admirer and collector of clocks and automata.

The emissaries must have initially thought that the bier in Abigail's death room, decorated with wreaths and garlands of white Damascene roses, and lit by dozens of flickering white candles, held not a dead child but a mechanical angel hammered from the finest metals—the world-famous automaton-builder's latest creation, ready at any second to rise up and open its eyes at the press of a button.

Cox had weighed down his daughter's eyelids with blue sapphires intended for a red kite commissioned by the Duke of Marlborough. He had covered her thin arms with the kite's silver wings. On her fever- and cough-ravaged body, wrapped in white Atlas silk, even the wings of a bird of prey shimmered like an angel's.

Cox had felt at that moment as if his own skin and facial expressions were made of metal, as if the temperature and slow trickle of his tears flowed down a statue in whose lightless interior he was imprisoned, when one of the two envoys, recognizing his mistake and realizing that he beheld not an automaton but a dead child, bowed deeply and sank to his knees beside the small corpse in the belief that this gesture was in keeping with a foreign custom.

In the intervening two years, Cox had thought of Abigail every hour of every day and given up building clocks. He could not bring himself to fashion a single cog, a single escapement, a single pendulum or balance at his work-bench, if each of these parts served only to measure the fleeting passage of time that not a gem in the world could prolong.

Five years, a meagre five years!, had been granted to Abigail from the riches of eternity. He had every clock removed, even the sundial on the south side of his house in Shoe Lane, after her small coffin had floated down into the darkness of a grave in Highgate cemetery—every clock apart from a single mysterious clock movement which he had inserted into Abigail's gravestone in lieu of a marble angel or a grieving faun.

He did not reopen his designs for this clock which was overgrown with ivy and roses within months, and which he had not even shown to Faye, until he sat at his workbench in China, searching for a mechanism capable, like an insect emerging from the cage of its cocoon, of spinning and spinning on itself and perhaps eventually out of time and into eternity. Cox had called the inconspicuous grave decoration, camouflaged according to the season by flowers, leaves or rosehips, Abigail's *life clock*, by which he might measure the passing of his own life and attune it to Abigail's eternal rest.

Cox's Liverpool, London and Manchester manufactories, where many hundreds of clockmakers and fine mechanics could give a chronometer the guise and voice of a blackbird or a nightingale, trilling a different song at noon, after dusk or at night, continued to build timepieces for royal households, ship owners and the Admiralty, but since Abigail's death this had been under the supervision of his friend and companion Jacob Merlin who now joined him at the rail. Jacob had often stood next to him in this manner over the past seven months on board, as if fearing that he might have to prevent Alister Cox, the saddest man in the world, from seeking peace in the dark ocean depths.

Are we really to land at Execution Dock? said Merlin. He too was holding a telescope.

Once, Cox had seen three buccaneers hanged at Execution Dock on the Thames on especially short ropes so that the fall from the scaffold did not break their necks as usual but, instead, left them to choke slowly to death under their own weight. The *pirate dance* was what spectators had called the men's thrashing as they vainly struggled for air: royal justice.

Cox shivered. Over the past two decades, the most illustrious households in England and on the Continent had placed orders with the office in Shoe Lane, some as gifts for themselves, others to win over more powerful or unconquerable courts such as the Russian Tsar's. But had any recipient of such a gift ever enquired after the creator of these clocks and automata, bestowed with pleas for trade clearance, Customs relief or other privileges?

The Emperor of China had.

When Cox had accepted Qiánlóng's invitation after two months of reflection and sent ink drafts of a kingfisher to Běijīng as a token of his consent, he had nourished high hopes that a journey to China might distract him from the inexorable advance of time and help him to return to building automata and perhaps even clocks—mechanical creatures that would, in truth, never be any more than toys. Peacocks, nightingales or leopards: toys for Abigail, twinkling with sapphires and rubies.

Like the princes, billionaires and warlords of Europe, the richest and most merciless individuals of their age, a godlike Emperor was now to be allowed to *play* in his throne rooms and audience pavilions with the miraculous beasts and dolls of a sleeping angel awaiting resurrection in the shade of a weeping pine in Highgate, and, in doing so, brighten his empire with a spark of childlike innocence.

DÀ YÙNHÉ

The Waterway

The Emperor did not want toys.

Neither the inhabitants of the villages and the licensed *water towns* on the banks of the Dà Yùnhé nor the crews of the thirty-five junks that had been sailing and rowing upstream from Hángzhōu for nine days now, past paddy fields and forests of mulberry and rosewood trees, could say which ship in this magnificent fleet was carrying His Holy Highness.

The junks, their sails emblazoned with constellations and golden dragons, and mounted on black pole masts, were almost indistinguishable. Their names too were to be concealed for weeks under red oilcloth until the warps were slapping against the quays of Běijīng. And in

16

a fashion unintelligible to the uninitiated, the order of the ships might change at any hour of the day or night without a single audible command. The seventeenth junk, for example, would glide past the ten ahead of it and take the place of the seventh while this ship slipped back into thirtieth place as the thirtieth advanced twenty positions and the first or fifth or ninth now brought up the rear, and so on.

No foe peering from cover on the rocky, overgrown, apparently peaceful green banks, no assailant or plotter should ever be able to identify which of the imperial ships he ought to target with his tar grenades, white-hot stone cannonballs or flaming arrows. He should not even be able to tell if this fleet really was transporting the Celestial One or if what was passing before his eyes under full sail was merely a grand feint.

The hours of day and night at which the fluid alterations to the fleet's formation took place were determined by means of flares and encoded flag signals from officers of the imperial guard posted on every junk. These guards were reported to have kept watch for the past thousand years: for every soldier who slept, a dozen had to stay awake.

Cox did not know if the Emperor was rocked to sleep night after night by the black waves of the Dà Yùnhé, the Grand Canal, or if Qiánlóng had not galloped off long ago, faster than any ship, across his fields, meadows and steppes under the protection of a squadron of armoured horsemen.

This river voyage would take seven weeks, maybe more, depending on wind and stopovers, and Qiánlóng had remained invisible since the sacrificial offerings— ghost money made from red rice paper—had fluttered through the air to mark the fleet's departure from Hángzhōu. He was invisible even as they passed large water towns where thousands of people lined the banks to cheer the fleet, and invisible too during the dramatic spectacle of junks being hauled on tow ropes via flooded wooden slipways up a gradient or over a dam by hundreds of water buffaloes and an army of slaves and servants to a deafening clamour of rain gongs, bells and horns.

Joseph Kiang, a Han Chinese born in Shànghǎi and baptized by a Portuguese missionary, had been assigned to translate for the English guests; he explained that the Emperor would appear like the first snowfall, like a hailstorm or a blazing summer's day. Everyone knew that not a year passed without snow, without storms or heat waves, but *when* the expected event might occur remained a probability wreathed in predictions and columns of astrological figures—a secret. Some servants and eunuchs, said Kiang, had lived at court for two or three decades without ever setting eyes on His Radiant Highness. After all, the only reason for a man to show his face was if he wished to face the world, leave his mark on it or measure himself with or against it.

Qiánlóng, on the other hand, could spend any river voyage asleep in a swaying bed or in a hammock woven from his enemies' hair, safe in the knowledge that no gradient, no torrent, no mountain and no distance, however great, could resist him. The most inventive hydraulic engineers had toiled for generations at his command and that of his dynasty to connect Běijīng to the delta of the Lán Chang Jiang and Hángzhōu, crafting complex lock systems to reverse the flow of tributaries, streams and springs until they converged into a single sparkling waterway.

The Dà Yùnhé was forty yards wide and the longest waterway dug by human hand. In places it was six fathoms deep, and almost one thousand two hundred miles long from Hángzhōu to Běijīng. There was no record of the number of servants, forced labourers and slaves who had perished from exhaustion, fever and injury or by the axes, arrows and daggers of rebellious clans over the centuries of muddy excavations for the Imperial Canal. Word in the water towns had it that there were one thousand dead for its every mile.

For the junks' crews and the hordes of helpers recruited in the villages on the banks and in the water towns, the successful negotiation of each gradient was a cause for celebration. Their breathless chanting as they strained in their harnesses to the rhythm of the gong mingled with the squawking of flocks of birds that darkened the sky—brent geese, cranes and grey herons; and whenever a junk finally slid into the smooth water of the next section of canal after hours of toil, and the reflected clouds split asunder, their many tugging songs would dissolve into cheers.

On evenings when the fleet's last ship had finally overcome the obstacle, huge fires were lit on the bank, and on them black-clothed cooks prepared the one hundred and eight courses of His Holy Highness's repast, as dictated by court custom. Yet the imperial fare from the smoking open waterside kitchens was not served to the Celestial One alone but also to all those who participated in his fleet's progress—for this crew, seven of the long series of dishes; for another, nine or ten or twelve of the one hundred and eight courses—each according to the meal's sustenance and the difficulty of the accomplished task.

The Celestial One insisted that his subjects dine with him—with him, the Invisible One, sharing one invisible table so that they might devour the fruits and bounty of the empire with his blessing. Even as the dishes were simmering in pots and pans and on spits, the cooks yelled out the names of all the ingredients and long lists of precious spices through brass megaphones, sometimes even associating, in verse, the cooking times and properties of a particular ingredient with the Emperor's powers which, like the heat of a campfire, wrought from raw materials and untamed elements an invincible empire with plentiful food for his subjects, a likeness of heaven.

Though Qiánlóng never appeared in person at a table or beside the large tarpaulins spread over the water meadows where the dishes were laid out between the flaming torches, still the diners, whether magnificently robed or half-naked and sweating from their labours in a towing harness, fell in, whooping, with the cooks' chants.

One time, the martial-sounding cheers struck Cox, who preferred to stay on the ship on such evenings, as a kind of war cry, and he sought in vain the signs of a coming battle.

Accompanied by Jacob Merlin and two assistants, a clockmaker from Dartford and a fine mechanic from Enfield, whom he had brought along on the greatest journey of his life for their exceptional skill and ingenuity, he had been welcomed to Hángzhōu like a royal guest from the barbarian West. The four pallid Englishmen, none of whom could understand, read or write the language of the empire, had been presented with silk rugs, splendid garments, white tea in lacquer boxes decorated with painted miniatures and virtually transparent porcelain worth its weight in gold in England. Yet none of them had seen the Emperor or a single one of his bodyguards.

Nevertheless, Kiang had said, His Radiant Highness held his sheltering hand over his guests at all hours of day and night. *Toys*. Kiang had indeed used the word toys—

the Emperor did not want toys—as he told Cox that it would be better to leave all the automata, the glittering pride of the *Sirius*'s cargo, in their cases and leather trunks aboard the barquentine. No one was allowed even to inspect these machines until the Emperor himself had laid his eyes upon them and then permitted others to take a look.

His Radiant Highness had other plans for his guests, Kiang had said, far greater plans. He did not wish to buy or trade or add to his artificial, mechanical menagerie. He had long since grown weary of mechanical creatures. Two shiploads of them, more than three-dozen automata delivered by the East India Company from England in the past five years alone! Enough, more than enough. No, the Emperor wanted their heads.

Our heads, a stunned Cox had asked, feeling a chill run down his spine. The horrible relic on his workbench in Liverpool lay before him again: a skull which, after much hesitation and under the pressure of overdue debt bonds, he had fashioned into the centrepiece of a pendulum clock for an Irish landowner. It was the skull of the former Lord Protector of England and archenemy of Ireland, Oliver Cromwell.

After slaughtering many thousands of Irish freedom fighters and their families, Cromwell had fallen into disgrace, though only posthumously, when his decomposed corpse was exhumed from Westminster Abbey and symbolically executed. His skull had been stuck on a pike and displayed on the top of a wall at Westminster Hall. Swarming with glistening flies, his grimacing face had stared out over the heads of the countless witnesses to a king's merciless punishment that extended beyond death itself until the Irish landowner, whose name Cox was never to learn, had someone steal and bleach the skull, then sent it to a secret workshop to have it incorporated into a clockwork that would count down every minute of the inexorable decline and fall of English rule.

Yes, your heads, Kiang had repeated with a bow to the English guest. Your head. Your ingenuity, your imagination, your skill for making mills that measure the course of time.

Mills? Cox had asked.

Clocks, the translator had said, correcting his mistake and raising both hands in apology. Clocks, automata, measuring instruments, machines . . .

And so, after three weeks at anchor in the roads, their time fully occupied with repairs to the rigging and hull, interrupted by downpours and high easterly and southeasterly winds, the *Sirius* had set sail again for Yokohama, taking with it the gleaming metal menagerie that represented virtually the entire assets of Cox & Co. And after initial dismay at seeing his business expectations thus dashed, Cox had stayed in Hángzhōu with Merlin and their two assistants, Aram Lockwood and Balder Bradshaw, in the hope that satisfying the Emperor's as-yet-mysterious wishes would perhaps produce an even greater profit than the sale of the *Sirius*'s cargo.

Resting in their cotton-wool and doeskin sachets, the metal creatures, powered by the finest hidden gears, could spread their wings or nod their silver heads in Yokohama or some other trading post authorized by the East India Company. Their beauty and agility delighted all who beheld them, and there would be buyers. After all, the mission assigned to the *Sirius* by the Royal Navy was not only to satisfy the wishes of the Emperor of China but also to explore the seas along the rim of the Pacific Ocean. In two years' time, at the latest by the autumn after next, the *Sirius* was to drop anchor again in Hángzhōu and take on board Cox and his companions, perhaps as rich men.

Who knows, said Merlin in an attempt to calm the two assistants from Dartford and Enfield, who were unsettled by the turn this business trip was taking, who knows, maybe Mister Cox would succeed, like an alchemist of grief, in transforming the numbing pain of his daughter Abigail's death into gold.

Cox saw many things in the weeks sailing with the fleet that would have moved him, in happier times, to spend whole nights sketching in his silk-covered cabin, drafting plans for rotating or wing-beating creatures, encrusted with emeralds or green amber:

Teams of water buffaloes drew carts and ploughs across paddies and fields, interspersed with patches of virgin forest, along the fertile banks of the canal, barely distinguishable from a slow-moving river. One sunny late October day, elephants laden with sacrificial offerings led a procession under fluttering banners from the walls and towers of a water town down to the water. These animals, smeared with honey and strewn with flower seeds, melon pips and wheat, Kiang had said, were among the last hundred specimens of the endangered Chinese elephant. Thronged with flocks of birds attracted by the honey, the seeds and the sweet pips, the elephants resembled thousand-winged creatures and it seemed as if their next pounding footstep might launch them into the air, along with their load of offerings—baskets filled with fruit and meat, incense and wreaths of flowers.

Another time, pink flamingos lined the fleet's route; or an endless column of water carriers bearing buckets dangling from bamboo poles made a promontory of brick-red earth look as if a human chain had brought it to life and it were flowering in time to the slow cycle of passing seasons . . . Mechanical sequences, programmed movements and clock-dial panoramas whichever way Cox turned his eyes.

But by the time the fleet reached Běijīng on one of the first frosty days of the year, he had forgotten these and other images of his voyage on the Dà Hùnyé, like a dream which fades within minutes of waking if it is not recorded in writing or words. The only memory he would retain was of one afternoon, as if the journey from Hángzhōu into the impregnable heart of the empire had lasted only that one afternoon. And that memory was the fleeting apparition of a girl. Or was it a woman? A girlish woman?

She was the only female Cox had seen on the junks. For though Kiang had said that the Emperor had brought one of his spouses and at least three hundred of his concubines along on this journey, the faces of the lovers and, all the more, that of an empress had to be protected from both the harmful rays of the sun, which accelerated the destructive passage of time, and any curious or covetous looks. The women rested below decks or read poetry, shielded from the gaze of the world and the sun by folding screens and canopies, listening to virtuoso musicians play cloud gongs or a moon guitar or simply to the bird and water music beneath the silence, or perfuming themselves and waiting, some calmly and quietly, other anxiously and full of secret dread, to be summoned to the Celestial One's bed.

To Cox, the farmers' wives, female fruit sellers and washerwomen on the jetties on the banks and in the fields had never been anything more than sexless figures in their wide conical rice-straw hats—models, perhaps, for the dial of a silver water clock. Yet the few seconds during which Cox had been permitted to see this girl stirred such a searing recollection of Abigail and her mother, his wife Faye, that for days he was sure that only a second encounter with this girl-woman on the deck could soothe his pain.

Faye had not spoken since Abigail's death. Barely out of childhood herself, over thirty years younger than Cox who had been struck by an all-consuming passion for her, she had become mute at their first and only daughter's deathbed, as if she had been no more than the shadow of a longed-for and now dead daughter, and had fallen silent with her, for ever.

Faye could no longer bear to sleep in the same bed, could not stand to be touched, would not respond to questions and asked none, would not even pronounce Abigail's name, wished to be alone when she ate, alone when she cut the bourbon roses in the garden and would tolerate no company on her long escapades through a city where, every day, women vanished without a trace—into brothels, cellars or simply into the blind waters of the Thames.

The withdrawal of such a painfully beloved person, to whom he had bound himself so closely, day after day, night after night, during their six years together that he had increasingly left his business dealings to Jacob Merlin, was a source of unprecedented torment to Cox.

Although he clung to the hope that one dark night in the future Faye would breathe easily by his side and in his arms, breathe easily while he awoke from this suffocating dream—only a dream; it would all have been a dream—the Chinese envoy's invitation strengthened his belief that he should perhaps leave Faye for the duration of an overseas trip to what she appeared to regard as the sole remedy for her pain: solitude; a life without him.

When, after months of contemplation, he finally accepted the invitation, he had to admit to himself that he could no longer bear to watch the most desirable creature he had ever met across an unbridgeable chasm—able to see her, but never to embrace or touch her. He imagined that the bond which tied him to Faye might grow tighter if he set out for Běijīng—grow tighter and tighter, slowly pulling his darling up and out of the speechless depths, black wells or wherever it was that she was imprisoned, out of his reach.

Besides arranging long-term contracts for his manufactories in Liverpool, Manchester and London, one of the most important features of his preparations for his travels to China was to give precise instructions as to how and where he should be sent news of Faye's return, details of the first words and the first sentence she spoke to enquire about him. He had also left sealed letters in Shoe Lane.

These testimonies of an overpowering yearning, his desire and his unwavering hope, were to greet Faye whenever fate, mollified by prayer and monetary offerings, chose to release her back into his love.

Faye and Abigail. As the fleet sped on gusty winds through a never-ending grid of paddy fields, as if dragging an enormous plough through fertile land by the sheer force of its sails, and as an inch-perfect manoeuvre sent a junk far back from its original position to the rear of the flotilla, the girl suddenly stood opposite him; she was standing at the bulwark of the passing, retreating junk, simply standing there, her crossed arms resting on a handrail—looking at him. And that same instant, a wave of memories, shadows, voices and sounds rose up from the black waters and the swaying green rice and transported Cox anticlockwise back in time into a grey haze where all he had lost was suddenly present again.

She was wrapped in a navy-blue coat embroidered with silver bamboo leaves, her hair pinned up with needles of glass or clear quartz, and she did not lower her gaze when Cox spotted her gliding past his junk, so close that if the two of them were now . . . were now to stretch out their arms, their fingertips would have met . . . No: the distance must have been greater, was definitely greater, but whenever Cox later recalled this encounter, this girl-woman came closer and closer until he thought that he might have embraced her across the streaming ribbon of water glittering beneath them in the afternoon sun.

However, it was only that coming, snowbound winter that he would discover her name and learn of all the obstacles and life-threatening taboos that protected her and those like her from any contact with a stranger. Her name was Ān.

From that first instant, Ān struck him as an incarnation of Faye *and* Abigail. It was not that she physically resembled his daughter or his wife, even if her face was as narrow as a European's and her eyes the same bright green and just as keen; even her hair was the same shade of black. Yet the bond was not a matter of colour or shape: it was her gaze, the unmistakable way in which those eyes scrutinized him and *how* they appeared to mirror a billowing sail, the river bank and the vast expanses of sluggishly passing fields, as if this woman had only to close her eyes and all reflections, objects and living things would disappear . . . Yes, that was it, that must have been it: it was as if that gaze was the origin from which every line of perspective in the visible world was derived.

A person capable of opening such eyes could create whatever she saw or make it vanish. If the Emperor of China claimed to be godlike, then the image passing before Cox's eyes that afternoon was a girl-woman who could, by her gaze alone, bring everything to life as well as cast it back into oblivion—a celestial being like Tian Hou, the goddess of the South China Sea, whose story Cox had heard in the past weeks aboard the *Sirius*: a fisher girl who had been made immortal, who was able to sink or save entire fleets from foundering, who could make even tarred masts blossom.

Abigail had looked at him this same way. Faye had looked at him from the depths of similar bright-green eyes, and, through the sheer bottomlessness of that gaze, in which the iris pigments shimmered like inclusions in the emeralds he sometimes inserted into his mechanical creatures for eyes, made him—Alister Cox, the most famous builder of automata that England had ever produced—her lover, her husband and the father of her only daughter; still more, her creation. He ran a constant risk of ruin if she were ever to lower her eyes or avert her gaze.

ZI JÌN CHÉNG

The Purple City

In thrall? Had Alister Cox been in thrall to his wife? Faye never imposed her will on him nor wanted anything from him—in any case, none of what Cox craved, night after night and throughout the day and whenever he was with her. Faye hadn't wanted him to kiss her or take her in his arms or rip off her clothes and bury her beneath him as a predator buries its prey . . . And she didn't want, had never wanted him to squirm and moan on top of her until, overcome with rage, pain and disgust, she felt his seed penetrate deep inside her, strike her to the core and then crawl out of her like a shapeless, watery bug, soiling her thighs and the bed sheet.

And yet she had admired the man, in the midst of his glittering mechanical creatures, who tormented her and, as he repeatedly whispered, as if begging for forgiveness, *worshipped* her, and even felt for him something she could only describe as love.

Three days after her seventeenth birthday, in a chapel flickering with the light of hundreds of candles and lapped, like a ship, by rolling waves of white chrysanthemums, white carnations and roses, Faye had become her father's employer's wife. As the eldest of five children born to a pious weaver woman and a one-legged Liverpudlian silversmith proud of having found a job in a Cox & Co. manufactory despite his crippled condition, neither her parents nor her bridegroom had asked for her opinion when they announced that her wedding day would be the happiest day of her life to date.

When she was still a child, unsteady in her straw clogs, Cox had sometimes thrown Faye up into the air, making her screech with laughter during those few thrilling seconds of flight, before catching her again, pressing her to his chest and kissing her on the forehead. Cox had always sought out Faye when he passed the lathes of the fine mechanics and silversmiths at his Liverpool manufactory, asking questions, proffering instructions and playing, here and there, with the children of a few privileged workers who were allowed, in winter, to bring their families to the workshops heated by coal-fired braziers.

Even though Faye struggled to recall those brief free-falls in later years, she retained a vague sensation from those times that this man made the impossible possible: flying. Flying! Fluttering silver birds, for example. Pieces of metal that twittered and sang. Dead materials, awakened to life.

After the wedding, Faye moved to London's Shoe Lane, into the brightest and most luxurious room she had ever entered; she visited her parents twice in her first year of marriage, bearing a gift hamper from her husband, and wept at luncheon both times while her mother laid a soothing hand over the fist in which Faye clutched her spoon, and her father cursed her for being an ungrateful princess. Hell's teeth! Was there any greater stroke of fortune for a snotty Scouse brat than to be transformed by blind and more-than-merciful Fate into the wife of a master like Alister Cox?

When Cox managed to tame his lust for his wife's girlish body and, of an autumn evening, as shooting stars leapt from the fire of great beech logs into the twilit living room and red wine sparkled in a carafe like molten garnet, explained to her how a sterling-silver barn owl beat its mechanical wings, Faye could occasionally be transformed back into an excited child and admire this man as she used to in his Liverpool workshops. And when barely an hour later she heard Cox grunting as he undressed and slumped into bed beside her, she whispered into her pillow an incantation her mother had taught her: A good heart. A good man. He has a good heart.

Abigail's birth in the first year of their marriage gave her hope for a while that there was happiness on the horizon somewhere—hope, in any case, as long as a perineal tear safeguarded her from her husband's lust, and even after her recovery, which eventually became impossible to delay or conceal, he approached her with greater caution than in nights before the birth. For Cox was beginning to discover by the side of a cherry-wood cradle, which almost engulfed this tiny new-born baby, an overwhelming sensation that seemed more powerful than his desire, stronger even than his enthusiasm for all things mechanical. And so even before she could articulate a word or babble her parents' names, his dearly beloved Abigail, his first and only daughter, built a bridge between Cox and Faye, spanning a gaping chasm and binding them together for five years—until whooping cough shattered that bond, and Cox lapsed into mourning, lustfulness and despair while Faye fell silent, seemingly for ever.

When the fleet reached Běijīng one ice-cold, cloudless late November day, glittering frost furred the leafless trees along the path decorated with golden brocade that led from the quayside into the centre of the world's largest city. The Almighty Ruler was carried to his residence in an endless procession of litters bristling with hundreds of silken banners and lances. Strangely, Cox was to find that

35

most secret place in the empire—and the most inaccessible to the vast majority of its subjects—so soothing, more familiar almost than any other staging post on his journey so far. *Zi jìn chéng*—the Emperor's Purple City. The Forbidden City.

That was because these gigantic expanses between the palaces and pavilions with their sweeping golden roofs and perfectly symmetrical buildings whose sonorous names Kiang translated as the *Palace of Earthly Tranquillity*, *Hall of Celestial and Terrestrial Union*, *Hall of Spiritual Nourishment* and *Pavilion of Pleasant Sounds* . . . these inch-perfect paths which appeared to have been traced with a yardstick, defining routes to which all residents, in accordance with his rank, must keep as strictly as if he were moving on a giant template spread across these broad courts—woe betide anyone who strayed even a pace from his allotted line! . . . these sundials, sandglasses and water clocks showing the times of day and night at which people must enter or leave a palace, a court or a garden, and the countless rituals, exercises and mysterious manoeuvres by the palace guards, determined by astronomical tables; all these things appeared to aid even someone as lost in his emotions and passions as Cox to find a way out of his turmoil and into a world of cast-iron order and, with it, a form of peace.

Although in this Purple City an army of slaves and servants, including no less than three thousand eunuchs at odds with their fate, could have testified that this place, opening its gates to the English guest, was no place of heavenly peace or terrestrial harmony, upon arrival Cox felt as if he had reached his goal.

The excruciating sense of unease that had once more befallen him when he finally left his junk and the forest of masts behind and was carried, rocking, towards the Forbidden City, surprisingly subsided when he had to take leave of Merlin and the two assistants at Tiananmen, *Square of Heavenly Peace*, which resembled a stone desert, swept clean of all urban life and even dust.

Only the master would reside in a guesthouse inside the Purple City. His assistants would be accommodated in a house outside the towering blood-red walls. Only Master Cox, said Kiang, would be, now and always, as close as possible to the thoughts of the Almighty, and spend his nights beneath the same tract of sky as His Sublime Majesty. The assistants would be escorted by guards through the West Gate to their master's workshop every morning, and back from the work benches to their lodgings every evening.

Like prisoners? asked Merlin.

Like cossetted, protected and esteemed guests, said Kiang, bowing.

And you? said Merlin, turning to Cox.

I will await you here, said Cox. Every day. As in Liverpool. As in London. As always.

As his litter was carried through the Gate of Heavenly Peace and past a three-rank honour guard into the echoing white emptiness of the forecourt, Cox wondered if somewhere inside these impregnable walls he would meet the delicate girl-woman he had seen standing at the railing as she floated past. He had told neither his companions nor Kiang about their encounter on the waters of the Imperial Canal, because his instincts warned him that it might be dangerous even to yearn for a woman who lived in the Emperor's shadow. But by chance, as the stony faces of the palace guard flashed past his litter, the memory of that apparition invaded his thoughts and brought him a fleeting sense of joy, for this image also contained something of the beauty of Faye's countenance and of Abigail's charm . . . until Cox's gaze alighted on the guardsmen's weapons—their black scabbards, their battle axes and spears trailing leopard tails, and their breastplates adorned with flames and lightning of jade and pink gold—and a chill came over him.

More even than the imperial splendour of the purple residence that lay like an island, surrounded by a deserted, cobbled expanse, a glacis of fear and awe in the heart of a roaring metropolis, what excited Cox the most that November day as Kiang led him through the luxurious guesthouse for his exclusive use was the sight of the adjoining workshop. It was a replica of his atelier in London, premises identical to his workshop in Shoe Lane. As Cox had knelt in despair beside Abigail's catafalque, keeping Qiánlóng's two envoys waiting and waiting, they must have made sketches and perhaps even taken measurements. This room could only have been built and furnished according to their drawings. Would he also find his and Faye's bed here? Abigail's bier?

A reproduction? He didn't know anything about that, Kiang said. And indeed the rest of the house, with its bamboo garden and a lotus pond lined with moss-clad stone, was as alien and delightful as any English visitor to the court of China could imagine.

And my companions? asked Cox. How were his companions' lodgings beyond the palace walls? And how far away?

Nearby, said Kiang. Out of earshot, but nearby. And their house had everything except for the lotuses, except for the pond.

But Cox didn't hear this. He had wandered from a living room decorated with burgundy wallpaper into the workshop through a wide door painted with tiger-hunting scenes, stopped alongside a lathe that must have been made in England, and thought of Abigail. If he were not expected to build something different, something completely different, at this workbench, then he would build a unique automaton for Abigail, a dragon spouting silver fog and fire, or a snail like the three-foot bronze sculpture he had seen on a plinth in the outer court.

Abigail had collected snail shells from under the rose-bushes in Shoe Lane, then painted them and kept them in a casket Faye had given her as a treasure chest. Yes, he would make a giant snail that could crawl across the tiles and walls of the palace, leaving a trail of pure silver behind it, and astonish the royal household no less than he was astounded by the Emperor of China's invisibility.

However, as Kiang guided the English guest the next day with an escort of four guards and a eunuch through the few lanes and forecourts of the Forbidden City that were open to visitors—mainly to point out to Cox the countless lines that he must never, ever cross—and Cox learnt that the only person permitted to move freely through this maze of invisible lines was the Emperor himself, snails and dragons and automata ceased to occupy his thoughts. The Emperor did not want toys. He wanted a clock. Maybe a clock. Why else would he have summoned a master craftsman from England?

Cox believed he understood that these rows of far-reaching courts and interlocking structures, artificial watercourses, shallow stone bridges and terraces that almost took flight, all measured and built according to the laws and proportions of the starry firmament, encased a courtly routine governed by heartbeats, breaths and prostrations as an engraved box houses a train of clock gears. And at the end of the tour, he thought that what he had seen resembled, more than anything, a gigantic stone clock movement, driven not by a pendulum but by an invisible heart, a concealed balance wheel without which not only this timepiece would come to a halt but also time itself: Qiánlóng.

A clock. He would present the Emperor with a clock which he, Merlin and the two assistants would build inside this palace, and which he would house in a snail, dragon or tiger cabinet made of a material more durable than the millennia. An indestructible beast of platinum, glass, gold and Damascus steel that did not merely measure time but also devoured it.

Merlin and the assistants had been uneasy, anxious even, when they parted with Cox outside the Gate of Heavenly Peace, but they were overjoyed when, the next morning, an escort in leather armour brought them to their master and his warm workshop with its capacious fireplace and enamelled brazier. The house they had been allocated seemed, indeed, to be every bit as comfortably furnished as their master's. Since the year was now turning chilly, coal-fired braziers, tended by two eunuchs, had been lit in each of the five chambers, and even the workshop here, with its charcoal that glowed without smoking and released an unidentifiable fragrance, was cosier than they had ever known winter to be at the lathes of the manufactories in Liverpool and London.

The master did have a lotus pond and rosebushes in a courtyard filled with birdsong, but his companions' house was built around a light well, panelled with carved wood, with a burbling fountain at its centre. None of them, not even Merlin, had ever lived in such splendour.

The only cause for concern here, said Lockwood, the silversmith, was that time would fly by too quickly and bring this blissful dream to a premature end. Bradshaw, the fine mechanic and second assistant, agreed with his friend: compared with England, this was paradise.

Did Cox & Co. treat you so badly then? asked Merlin, handing him a kind of map of the city on which a sinuous red line traced their daily route to work, from the assistants' house through the West Gate to the workshop.

Well? Did Cox & Co. treat you so badly?

Yet the excitement of the silversmith Aram Lockwood and the fine mechanic Balder Bradshaw seemed already to have subsided. They were no longer laughing but looked sheepishly at the floor where a column of ants was struggling to drag a lead-grey moth, which was offering only weary, hopeless resistance, back to their colony for food.

The column of ants must still have had some distance to cover, because the lacquered floor was as smooth as glass and no entrance to the underworld was to be seen.

WÀN SUÌ YÉ

Lord of Ten Thousand Years

The snow came early that year, to the horror of some
priests in the Purple City, who saw it as an evil omen; it
fell in feather-sized flakes from a blue sky. Although the
court astrologers had predicted to the Emperor that the
weather would be mild and sunny for the open-air performance of an opera composed by a twelve-year-old prince,
and although roses were still blooming in the palace gardens, one morning the wind veered from west to north.
Then the eerie snow began to fall. At first, individual flakes
came tumbling down out of the blue sky, as if they had
strayed from a remote season, then they fell more and
more densely before finally coalescing into a blizzard
impenetrable to the eye, obscuring lanes, squares, pavilions
and palaces.

By the time the snowfall subsided as unexpectedly as it had begun after barely an hour, the Forbidden City lay wrapped in a cold white mantle which had not only erased every other colour but also muffled voices and other sounds. In this magical silence, the sun once more rode high over the snow-covered palace roofs and made the snow crystals and gold sparkle on the meltwater-rinsed roofs.

It was only some weeks later that a rumour, rife with contradictions, spread through the Purple City, and eventually the lanes of Běijīng, that it had been the astrologers—the astrologers!—who had tried to ward off an imminent refutation of their favourable weather forecast by filling firework rockets with silver salt and firing them for an entire day at the unmoving wall of cloud from the summits of the Shan mountains. The silver salt scattered high in the sky above the peaks was meant to burst the fists of cloud and cause the rain, hail, snow and whatever else they might hold to pour, hail or snow far from the city and, most importantly, far from His Sublime Majesty's sight.

Yet, as if attracted by the firework bouquets scrawled as palely as watermarks in the day-lit sky, a gusty wind had risen to the sound of the echoing explosions rebounding from the rock faces and the gorges of the Shan mountains, compacting the snow showers still hanging high above the ground and driving them into the skies over the Forbidden

City where, at last, they released their crystalline cargo to fall to earth.

Shortly before the blizzard, Cox had seen a double rainbow arching over the roofs of the Purple City and believed that the colourful spectacle he saw in a cloudless sky was a climatic phenomenon specific to the latitude of Běijīng. But then, in the face of a wave of icy air rolling in ahead of the first snow flurries, he had withdrawn to the hearth of his house. When the sky cleared and a cold sun shone forth once more, he went outside and admired a glittering city, glittering roofs and glittering, dazzling white courts, utterly pristine.

In the days that followed, Jacob Merlin, Aram Lockwood and Balder Bradshaw appeared for work at their master's house every morning with an escort of silent guards and were accompanied home every evening without Cox having answered their questions as to what exactly they were supposed to produce in the pleasant warmth at their workbenches. Following their rejection, the treasures and shimmering automata that the *Sirius* had carried so many thousands of sea miles had been floating across the South China Sea for many weeks and would find no buyer until Yokohama.

The weather remained sunny, but had turned windy and icy cold. It was whispered that the Emperor had taken the snow as a sign that the composer prince should use his perfect pitch, improve his opera and postpone its performance until he had achieved the highest level of perfection—and that might be why he had chosen not to punish the astrologers just yet. They ventured no further predictions and begged on their knees to a mandarin, whose robe was embroidered with two golden leopards as a symbol of his exalted rank, for patience: an overcast sky and autumn fog prevented them from reading the stars.

The snow retreated only slowly from the shady courts. Meltwater dripped from the mouths of dragon-headed waterspouts on the roofs at the earliest around midday, and the gurgling ceased again in the early afternoon.

In the white, almost cheerful wintery light which fell through the workshop's window, Merlin ordered the clock- and automaton-building material and tools they had brought with them in trunks, cases and chests to be tidied away, arranged and readied for an imperial assignment about whose nature even Kiang could only speculate. There was still no signal from His Sublime Majesty's entourage. The deep silence surrounding the Emperor seemed to grow even heavier with the fear of the astrologers who were afraid that they might still, one day, be punished for their erroneous forecast.

The Emperor loved windless, dry and bright weather because he enjoyed listening to songs, choirs and tinkling orchestras in his gardens, or at least out in the open air. Only then could he experience the sensations of the opera while also observing the procession of the clouds and, when the orchestra and singers fell silent for a few bars, hear the sound of the wind in the rose bushes, the whisper of bamboo leaves and the symphonic music of wild nature tamed by human hand.

Yet the Emperor may have lost patience during the long wait for weather conditions that were to his liking, and he blamed these tiresome circumstances on the astrologers. Was it not outrageous that an Almighty Ruler who loved still air and the carefree passing of the clouds could not simply tear apart the leaden, overcast skies above his residence and strew their tattered remains to the four winds? A culprit for this outrage had to be found, someone to blame, and hence the astrologers trembled.

The English guests learnt more and more about the objects of His Sublime Majesty's affection, scorn and contempt from Kiang who repeated and translated court gossip for them. Yet what was expected of the English master craftsman appeared to be a secret, even from the most garrulous informers. Had Qiánlóng lost interest in the skills of his English guests? Or simply forgotten them? After all, the

Lord of Heaven and Earth bore the weight of the world through the ages at the same time as he considered endless lists of questions, so it was possible that entire armies might slip his mind.

But Cox did not appear remotely troubled. Indeed, he struck his companions as being utterly certain and free of doubt, as if he knew exactly what Qiánlóng expected of him and of them all, and was merely waiting for permission to speak to the others about it and not just to himself. For speak he did, and indeed sometimes whispered to himself. Yet when Merlin asked, Are you talking to me? Are you talking to us? Cox did not answer. When the two assistants thought nobody was watching and their eyes met, one or other would tap his forehead: He's gone mad.

For his part, Kiang did not tire of preparing the English guest for his impending audience with the Emperor, demonstrating to Cox the number and kind of genuflections required and how to touch his forehead to the ground, and tying squares of felt around his knees with leather thongs to protect him from the cold and the chill hardness of the floor in case the audience took place in the Palace of Heavenly Tranquillity, one of the seven pavilions in which the Emperor received his subjects.

When the time came, Cox was to wear a long red robe like a mandarin so that nobody would see the felt squares that traditionally provided relief to high-ranking subjects required to genuflect before His Sublime Majesty. And no yellow under any circumstances! said Kiang. No gold. Nothing from head to toe that even remotely resembled a colour exclusive to the Emperor. After all, only the sun emitted rays of this colour, none of its planets.

What about the moon?

Oh, even if the moon occasionally hung in the night sky with a golden glow, all it did was reflect the sun which lent the moon some of its glory in the darkest hours, as His Sublime Majesty did to his subjects.

Wàn sui yé, said Kiang, was the title that a kneeling Cox should employ if the Emperor happened to ask him a question. This had been decided by the First Cabinet of Court, responsible for audiences. *Wàn sui yé*: Lord of Ten Thousand Years. That was what the three thousand eunuchs in the Purple City called their lord: Wàn sui yé, even if they never saw him; Wàn sui yé, even if they were merely talking about him or dreaming of his clemency.

Cox had his assistants cut cogs, escapements and plates of all shapes and strengths from English rolled sheet metal; he had them file, saw and polish so that whatever the forthcoming audience might hold, no assignment would take him by surprise. But his assistants secretly interpreted the growing arsenal of components for the most varied kinds and sizes of clock movements as a sign that the master himself was unsure what tasks to set himself and his men.

Kiang urged them to be patient. Even His Sublime Majesty's closest confidants were incapable of deciphering his wishes and thoughts, since a predictable ruler could all too easily become the plaything of intrigue or a conspiracy.

Even his closest confidants were incapable of deciphering his plans? So he has confidants? asked Merlin as Cox ran his eyes over an island of snow in the court outside the workshop's south-facing window. There were no tracks in the snow.

Advisers, said Kiang, correcting himself. His advisers. At the apex of the world, there was no room for confidants.

Cox stepped closer to the window. A procession of litters, shaped like boats or magnificent gondolas, emerged from the shadow of the wall beyond which, Kiang had explained, lay the Women's Palace. Twelve, fourteen, sixteen of them, Cox counted, a sparkling golden fleet swaying in the hands of their bearers across the snow island's immaculate whiteness. The bearers' terracotta-coloured robes identified them as eunuchs. Although the procession was advancing at walking pace across the court and the island of snow towards a gate studded with golden thorns that led into the innermost regions of the Purple City, it was not taking the shortest, most direct route, describing instead a curving path through the dazzling light according to a rule known perhaps only to the leading eunuch.

The circuitous path the eunuch was stamping into the snow was possibly a detour that the astrologers had determined in order to avoid an ambush laid by an invisible demon. Maybe, however, this curve merely signified that the straight path, the most direct and seemingly shortest path into the Forbidden City, usually led to perdition.

The hindmost litters were still rocking along in the shadow of the walls and the foremost were already moving across the island of snow when a piercing cry brought the procession to a halt. One of the bearers of the fourth litter had fallen. He was now kneeling in the snow, hunched over and clutching his chest with his arms, as if trying to prevent his lungs or his heart from bursting while the litter listed slightly like a boat run aground.

Cox's first thought was that the man's effort had made him vomit, for the glittering pomp of the litters must surely weigh more than any passenger, but then he saw the man cough up a stream of blood and then another, and heard, if only remotely and indistinctly through the closed workshop window, the retching, barking splutter as the snow was stained red, deep red, in front of the kneeling man.

Then the fallen porter collapsed face first into the middle of his bloodstain without loosening his self-embrace, and lay motionless. The procession of gondolas stood silent and unmoving behind them. The bearers of the first three litters and their eunuch guide had continued for a few steps before the hoarse coughing made them look back and stop.

The bloodstain in the snow seemed to have transformed the gap between the short vanguard and the long tail of the procession into a horror scene none of the following party could cross. Which litter bearer, which invisible passenger would risk the iniquity of deviating from a minutely measured and determined route to come to the aid of a dying man?

Although Merlin, Kiang and the two assistants were so absorbed in conversation that they had neither heard nor seen the events unfolding in the enormous court outside the workshop window, Kiang at least must have suspected something from the English master's facial expression. One after another, with Kiang taking the lead, they had joined Cox by the window. They were silent witnesses to the frozen procession of litters in the snow, the bearer sprawling in a pool of his own blood and the bewildered paralysis of the fleet of gondolas.

Only Cox's gaze had moved on, much further on, his eyes spellbound by a slender, almost childlike hand, which had appeared between the folds of one of the litters' crimson curtain and was now drawing it aside. A woman's hand. It was the second litter back from the bloodstain. Maybe the passenger had wished to cast a glance out from the dim, perfumed, comfortable interior into the life of a servant surrounded by blinding light—and now saw his death. Maybe, though, her other, still-invisible hand already rested on an ivory knob that opened the gondola door. Maybe she would step out onto the crusted snow and care for the motionless man, or at least break the spell weighing on the procession and call for help.

Cox had followed these events outside the window with a strange absence of emotion, the way he might have watched a staged portrayal of a litter-bearer's death. It was what happened next that brought home to him the power of real life. This hand . . . This hand and the two stones spitting white flamelets of varying brilliance and clarity on the knuckles of a delicate middle and ring finger: one might be a white topaz hatched with silver needles of rutile, the other an uncut diamond, gleaming like a lump of sugar in a white-gold setting. What strange and singular ornaments. Cox, who had seen great piles of gemstones spilling over his workbenches, had noticed these differing glows back on the Imperial Canal, back at the rail of the junk, and was sure that this hand could only belong to the woman, or girl, who had slid past him on the waters of the Dà yùn hé, reminding him, like a two-faced creature, of his silent wife and lost daughter. Would this creature— half-daughter, half-desirable woman—climb down from the litter and bend over the motionless man? And in doing so would she perhaps feel the gaze from the workshop window, his gaze, and turn towards him as she set foot on the snow?

And then, as if this really were the end of an act in a play, a blind painted with lotus leaves came clattering down in front of the window, replacing the wintry view outside with embroidered flowers, a kingfisher, reeds and scudding clouds. Kiang had pulled the sash of the blind, and anything still visible beyond the window was obscured from them.

In the Forbidden City, said Kiang, in the city of His Sublime Majesty, nothing may be seen, indeed nothing may become visible other than that which the court laws graciously allowed the eyes to behold. Anything unexpected or unpredicted must be removed from the sight of non-participants, let alone strangers, until the relevant councillors, with the Almighty Ruler's approval, had authorized them to see it.

And beware! Beware! Forbidden gazes had occasionally been punished on the very day of their crime by blinding—by pushing into the culprit's orbits an open pair of *eye-gougers* whose blades could be adjusted to the features of every subject in the empire. Or by passing a white-hot dagger blade just in front of the pupils, bringing the orbits to a boil. Or by the executioner pouring a trickle of molten lead into the voyeur's sockets.

People fall over in the snow, collapse under their burdens, said Cox. People die. Is it forbidden to look upon life in this city? Is a fallen servant a forbidden sight?

He had not noticed if someone had fallen and knew nothing of what had happened nor who was being carried in those litters, said Kiang, but whatever might have occurred, the English guests should trust him: it could only be bad for their eyes.

When Cox pulled up the blind at dusk, the assistants and Kiang had left, and the court once more lay broad and empty before him. Even the island of snow had vanished, as if the events had never happened or every trace and memory of it had been erased and eradicated. Late that night, after a vain attempt to continue writing a journal that he one day intended to read aloud to Faye, he lay there on pillows decorated with constellations, unable to sleep, and Faye's and Abigail's faces repeatedly blurred and intermingled with the features of the girl or woman at the railing.

Wàn sui yé: Lord of Ten Thousand Years. Cox began to recite the official title like a charm to fend off these drifting, fleeting faces. Kiang had recommended this exercise to him and had demonstrated, in the form of a slow dance, how everyone, from Cox to the mightiest mandarin, had to kneel before His Sublime Majesty, touch the ground with his forehead, stand up and then genuflect again, three times in succession, in order to feel, for the span of three breaths, the coolness of the ground and the dust to which His Sublime Majesty could grind anyone who did not live up to his expectations.

Wàn sui yé. First Cox had whispered the name of Lord of Ten Thousand Years, then, as he succumbed to creeping fatigue, had merely imagined it, just as, when he was a child and couldn't sleep, he had silently counted swallows darting in speeding spirals against what seemed like a dream-like sky . . . He was imagining that he was far, far up in a dazzling white swallow-filled sky when he felt a hand on his shoulder. It was Kiang. It was dark and cold. The brazier had gone out. Stars he had never seen before twinkled through the windows of his bedroom. It was pitch black, the small hours of morning.

Wàn sui yé.

Wake up, Master, said Kiang, then as the drowsy man turned away from him and threatened to sink back into a dream, he repeated, Wake up, Master Cox. The Lord of Ten Thousand Years wishes to see you.

SHÍ JIĀN

A Man

Now he too was swaying in a litter through the darkness.
Cox sat beside Kiang in that cramped silk-lined space, as
if the gondola procession of the previous day had pursued
him around a long curving path through the snow and the
empty courts and into his dreams, had finally caught him,
picked him up and carried him back into the reality of this
black morning. Shivering, he noticed something that must
be fear growing and spreading inexorably through him.
For it was one thing to have heard of a man with the
power to determine life and death without ever encoun-
tering an obstacle or an objection—and quite another to
face that man and fall to one's knees before him.

It was strange, but in the envoys' speeches in London,
peppered with bows and elegant gestures, the Emperor
of China had come across as a beaming, magnetic and

ultimately enticing vision. Now this vision conjured up an invisible and all-powerful being, and Cox was at the mercy of the will and moods of a despot obsessed with clocks and automata, who could kill him with a single word or gesture whose meaning Cox would presumably only grasp in the last fatal moment.

After Kiang had woken him, it had taken a while for Cox to shake off his drowsiness in the bedroom lit by a saffron-coloured lantern, and come to the realization that what he had sailed halfway around the world for, and what he and his assistants had waited for in vain for so long, was now truly coming to pass. A man who had elevated himself far above the rest of humanity as Ruler of the World, His Sublime Majesty, the Almighty, the Lord of Ten Thousand Years and countless other titles and names, would express a wish that he would either fulfil or fail to satisfy—and maybe die. For the wish of the Ruler of the World and the Lord of the Horizons was a command, brooking neither hesitation nor failure.

Cox tried to push the litter curtain aside. Kiang made no attempt to stop him. However, the fabric was interwoven with silver threads, thick as a rug and fastened to the doorframe by tacks with heads representing tigers or leopards. It might have just about been possible to tear off or cut through this screen, preventing passengers from being seen but also from seeing, but it could not be opened without force.

Where are they taking us? asked Cox, expecting to hear the name of one of the audience pavilions whose splendour Kiang had already described to him with reverential passion.

Where? said Kiang. You know where. To Him.

Kiang, assisted by a companion whom Cox had never seen, had transformed the English guest's bedroom into a dressing room and the Emperor's guest into a mandarin. There, Cox put on a precious red robe with white fur trimming and wide hanging sleeves and boots made of silk studded with moonstones. His hair was combed back severely with scented oil to give the impression, to one sitting or standing opposite him, that a plait cascaded down his back. His neck and his hands were perfumed, and felt pads were attached with leather straps to his knees to ward off the cold and hardness of the stone floor of an audience hall whose name even the litter-bearers would not discover until an officer of their escort whispered it to them. Pieces of fabric depicting two silver pheasants taking off had been skilfully stitched to the front and back of Cox's robe.

The Emperor, Kiang had said, did not wish to tire his eyes with the sight of European clothing which, however fashionable and expensive it might be, concealed only the ridiculous nudity of a naked white man, and was, at best, a display of wealth by an otherwise-insignificant costumed individual.

The robe of a mandarin, on the other hand, reflected—like a eunuch's brown tunic—a rank and a role assigned to a person not only in his own society and time or in the Forbidden City but also in the universe. And that he, Cox, was to appear before the Emperor as a dignitary, dressed in the silver-pheasant robe of a high official, was a sign of the Emperor's forbearance and favour: the Lord of Ten Thousand Years was elevating him and bringing him closer to his throne.

Was it purely due to the morning chill, or to the dwindling distance, as the litter-bearers' every step carried him closer to an Almighty Ruler who could, with a single flick of his wrist, propel one of his subjects a hundred ranks higher or have him trampled under the boots of his guardsmen or hacked to pieces by their battle axes? In any case, Cox began to tremble as he withdrew his hand from the double litter's nailed-down curtain. If what Kiang had said yesterday by the workshop window were true, then he and his companions had seen something that was not for their eyes and for which any inhabitant of the Purple City could be blinded. Was he perhaps being carried not to an audience but to a court which, like many places in this world where the harshest penalties were handed down, executed its sentences in the earliest hours of the morning, at a time remote from people's daily lives and barely distinguishable from night? Had Kiang informed on Cox's criminal, forbidden gaze with the intention of gaining a promotion closer to the light of the throne?

Cox didn't know if other litters were being carried through the darkness ahead of and behind him. The cordon of guardsmen that had surrounded him and Kiang, shoving rather than guiding them from the vestibule of his house to the litter and now presumably running alongside, had been so dense that he had seen nothing but the black of morning beyond the armoured shoulders and over the plumed helmets. The litter had swallowed them like a shimmering, silent beast running through the night, its stomach replete with its prey. The only sounds audible above the bearers' footsteps were the boots of the guard and the occasional, oddly melodious jangling of their weapons or armour.

A great favour, Kiang repeated, but his voice sounded nervous, even anxious in a way Cox hadn't previously remarked in a man who was never shy to offer advice or explanation.

Had Kiang ever been face to face with the Emperor, seen him at close quarters?

Kiang seemed to be preoccupied, or had simply decided to ignore Cox's question.

Kiang. Had he ever been face to face with the Emperor?

Kiang said nothing.

On your knees! On your knees, Master Cox! For pity's sake, on your knees! were the first words Cox heard his companion utter a few minutes later.

The litter had been set down on a guardsman's whispered commands in front of a dimly lit, dark-red lacquered portal inlaid with two man-sized golden ideograms. As if every motion needed to be perfectly synchronized with all others, the inscribed gates began to swing inwards with a gentle sigh at the precise moment a eunuch opened the litter door and, his hand still on the doorknob and his arm outstretched, bowed to Kiang who stepped under the porch of the pavilion and beckoned to Cox.

Shimmering with lustrous gold lacquer and silk in the flickering light, the hall stretching out before them beyond the open gates—its dimensions seemed truly gigantic to Cox—obviously had only one purpose:

The throne, which stood not at the end but somewhere just beyond the middle of the hall, was surrounded by a room of genuinely terrifying depth—an expanse filled with a metallic gleam that anyone who wished to approach the throne was obliged to cross. This gave the armoured warriors—helmeted, plumed shadows standing as still as statues along walls hung with tapestries embroidered with writing—a great deal of room and an awful amount of time to prevent anyone who approached the Almighty Ruler from launching a suicidal attack, making a wrong move or pronouncing an unwise word, and to bury him under their armour.

On your knees! On our knees, Master Cox!

Kiang whispered or rather breathed his order almost beseechingly as he fell to his knees. Cox looked up at the still-remote throne before copying him and sinking to the ground, bowing lower and lower, pressing his forehead to the floor, rising up again onto his knees and, as instructed, standing up and sinking down again, three times in succession, in order finally to listen for the quiet, almost inaudible voice of the most powerful man on Earth, a god. A wide silk carpet, its finely woven pattern of waves, surf and reflected light presumably representing a river or the moat of an impregnable fortress, separated the place of genuflection from His Radiant Highness's location.

But the throne was empty.

Strangely squat, it stood, gleaming gold, on a raised dais reached by three low steps in the middle of the river of woven carpet. At the ends of its broad upholstered arms were dragon's heads which seemed to spout light from their gaping jaws. The back of the throne consisted of the intertwined jade-green bodies of dragons. Curiously modest, perhaps because only three steps separated it from the same floor that ordinary subjects trod, this symbol of absolute power did not loom above everything else; it merely stood there.

On your knees! Silently, his heart pounding, Cox knelt beside Kiang at a point measured to the very inch from the throne. The guards arrayed along the walls cast long shadows across the empty centre of the hall. Apart from the fragrant clouds of incense rising from the capitals of four pillars around the throne and then drifting away on sluggish draughts, the restless shadows of the warriors were the only thing moving in the silence.

And now Cox heard a voice and he was certain from the first instant that it was the sound of the Emperor's voice. And despite his racing pulse, he could barely suppress a disbelieving smile, which twisted into a grimace in his desperate attempt to hide it from the empty throne, as amid this mysterious lustre and sophisticated splendour which consisted largely of gentle reflections and seemed to Cox as alien as the glow of a shrine on a distant planet, Kiang translated the Emperor's words for him:

A platitude of such banality that it would not have sounded out of place at the bar of a tavern by the Thames; a vacuous phrase that had nonetheless, indisputably, been uttered by that voice in the abstract, distant twilight beyond a screen also covered with characters inscribed by a virtuoso calligrapher at the height of his powers. How time flies!

How time flies!

Had the Western world's most famous clockmaker and automaton-builder sailed halfway around the world and up an artificial river, dug by millions of slaves, to Běijīng, and then spent an entire autumn at a court whose existence was merely a fantastical rumour to most inhabitants of the West, waiting for a word from the Emperor of China, all to kneel before an empty throne and hear this cliché?

However, the voice behind the screen went quietly on, inserting pauses of varying lengths that left barely enough time for a translation, while Kiang anxiously pricked his ears, searching for terms to convey His Sublime Majesty's words in a barbarian language. How time flies, Kiang translated hastily between two apparently irregular silences that the Emperor had left him to perform his transformational exercise.

How time flies, said or rather whispered the Emperor repeatedly during his speech in the twilight; but whether it crawls, stands still, flies or overwhelms us with one of its countless changes of gear depends on us and on the instants of our lives that interlock like links in a chain.

Might a man sentenced to death, the final hours of whose life are racing past, not have whiled away those same hours in idleness and soporific boredom in a riverside garden on a summer's afternoon, with dragonflies buzzing around him, if he had not committed a crime?

And what about a child, a single one of whose infant years seems to stretch on for all eternity, and who dreams that the passage of time will accelerate, carrying it closer to the supposed liberties its parents enjoy? It must experience how the minutes of a particular afternoon suddenly start to race as it waits for the punishment its father is sure to administer when he returns home that evening.

Then again, two lovers hope on the cusp of daybreak that it might be the song of the nightingale that roused them from their light slumbers after their many pleasures—only the nightingale, not the morning call of the lark. Thus love, more than anything else, seems to raise two people high above all notions of time into a realm where the hours do not pass in a trickle but entirely cease to flow.

And if someone devotes himself utterly to his imagination, his own creations and passions, the sun can rise and set again without his noticing its passing.

Yet though a man nurtures the boundless belief . . . (here it was Kiang who marked a long pause, as if to repeat the Emperor's words filled him with dread) . . . though a man harbours the belief that he is the Lord of Time, it still flows more quickly with each completed year while so many other aspects of his life become lethargic and slow. No sooner has he gathered his loved ones around him to mark festivities than another year has passed, and, gradually, he begins to resemble a condemned man awaiting his execution day.

Shi jiān, shi jiān. Cox thought he heard over and over again during this monotonous, sermon-like speech the words *shi jiān*, or something similar. *Shi jiān*, said the voice behind the screen. Time, said Kiang, translating. Time, the course of time, measurable time—*shi jiān*.

But Cox was hardly listening to either of them now. The sounds of two languages in the invisible presence of the most powerful man in the world made him drowsy, and yet he was completely alert:

Time. Time! Good heavens, this sermon went on and on. Daybreak. His eyes fixed unwaveringly on the empty throne, Cox felt rather than saw the first glimmer of daylight slowly shrinking the dimensions of the hall whose edges had moments earlier been part of the never-ending darkness. Almost imperceptibly at first, the growing brightness caused his attention to slacken. His attention! The Emperor of China was addressing him and Kiang was taking reverential and even anxious pains over the translation, but to Cox the voice from behind the screen, Kiang's words and the daybreak had receded to the margins, a sense of triumph had gripped the English guest:

He *knew* what Qiánlóng was thinking, knew what Qiánlóng would say! He knew what the Emperor of China wanted from him before he could pronounce it and Kiang could translate his desire. It was as if Cox could feel the strings that directed the movements of a puppet, hidden behind the screen and behind the claims of omnipotence, tightening in his fingers. Who knows, maybe beyond that magnificent screen covered with ideograms there was indeed nothing but an automaton whose mechanism and motions Alister Cox, the world's greatest machine-builder, had no trouble identifying.

As Kiang continued his faltering translations, the throne room brightened. Cox felt the cold floor through the felt pads fastened to his knees beneath the wide folds of his mandarin's robe.

Kiang was still speaking when Cox realized from the shadows and sounds behind the screen that His Sublime Majesty was now retiring, leaving the translator to communicate his will and instructions to the English guest.

Cox was tempted to tell Kiang that he need trouble himself no further, that he already knew what the Emperor wanted from him and that Kiang could explain the rest back at the workshop, but the two kneeling men were still waiting for a signal that would authorize them to stand up, stride backwards across its great, dawn-lit expanse, still bowing deeply to the empty throne, and leave. With this signal—three or four words, which Kiang did not translate, from an equally invisible master of ceremonies standing in the shadow of the guards—the men were released from their now excruciating pains but only after long minutes of silence.

It was that easy. But was everything really that easy? The Emperor wanted Cox to build him clocks to measure the racing, creeping or frozen times of a person's life; machines to show the cycle of the hours or the day according to the subjective experience of a lover, a child, a condemned man and other people trapped in the chasms or cages of their lives or floating in bliss above the clouds—the variable tempo of time.

And yet, as Cox and every clock-making apprentice knew, slowing or speeding up the passage of time was simply a matter of adding or removing a few cogs, the length of the pendulum, escapements and mechanical parts that any engineer worth his salt could assemble into a clock movement.

The presence of brass cogs of varying size and number could make time fly—inside a clock movement, at least—or reduce it to a snail's pace. Anyone able to construct a mechanism of this kind, capable of reproducing the speeds of a wide range of different circumstances, would, by dint of his clockwork—like a puppet master's strings controlling his puppets' virtual fate—rise to the rank of Lord over Time, and make it either fly past or bring it to a standstill.

But were an Emperor's wishes really so easy to satisfy, his thoughts so easy to read, even when he concealed his appearance behind a screen decorated with painted words?

Although Cox began to question his intuition even as the litter-bearers carried him and Kiang back to his quarters and workbench, and Kiang merely confirmed what he had understood during the audience, he was sure that he, Alister Cox, could read the thoughts of the Emperor of China, the thoughts of an ordinary man—provided, at least, that that man was talking about the course of time and clocks.

Yet Cox also knew that this realization was the most precious possession he had ever owned, and that he must guard this ineffable secret from Kiang and even from his companions if he ever wanted to make it back to London and there tell Faye, his unrequited love, his silent wife, that the godlike Emperor of China was human too.

6

HÁI ZI

The Silver Ship

If the almighty Qiánlóng wished to measure the tempo of time for different episodes of a person's life and build the appropriate clocks without instructing his English guest with which time and which clock to commence his work—the time of lovers, the dying or a child?—then Cox had not a second's hesitation in deciding which timepiece he and his assistants would craft during his first winter in the Purple City.

The first Chinese character of many that Cox learnt to hear, write and pronounce, and which he would eventually, at a moment's notice, even when startled from a dream, be able to paint on a board or trace, like a soft engraving, with his finger on a pillow, in snow or in sand, was *Hái zi*.

Somewhat clumsily at first, but then to Kiang's satisfaction, it took Cox only two lessons to learn to write the character in ink on a large sheet of rice paper which he later pinned to the wall above his workbench. *Hái zi*. It meant *child*. The child.

Hái zi. The Almighty had given him the choice.

The fact that the Emperor did not choose himself but left someone else to do so, what is more a foreign guest at his court, said Kiang, a guest who might disappear one day, denying all responsibility, was something that neither he nor anyone else entitled to set foot in the Forbidden City had ever witnessed before.

Yet if someone wants everything, said Cox, *everything*, then is it not wise of him to leave the decision about where to start to the person who will, some day, have to lay it all at his feet?

Were you able to understand this court, its signals and its languages, Master Cox, said Kiang, then you would realize you are mistaken. That the Lord of Ten Thousand Years and the Lord of All Decisions has given you this choice—any choice—is a riddle only a god can solve.

But Cox had fallen silent.

The child. A child's time. So Cox would build for his patron, as a first demonstration of the variable passage of time, a clock that would reproduce and measure the wave-like forward motion, the rushing rise and fall, the leaps and dives and moments of gliding flight and even standstill in a child's lifetime. Yet that he would think of only one child as he worked, a child who rested beyond the reach of space and time, and by doing so elevate the memory of his daughter Abigail above even a lord who ruled over ten thousand years, was just one of the many secrets that Alister Cox would have to keep throughout the hard times of his stay in the Forbidden City.

It hadn't snowed again since the first onset of winter and the procession of litters when the girl-woman had floated past Cox for the second time. The courts were bare, flecked here and there with the odd scrap of snow, under an often-cloudless sky. Some mornings the grimacing gargoyles on the roofs bristled with hoarfrost.

It was often so soporifically warm at the Englishmen's workbenches, however, that Cox had servants keep only one of the three braziers alight. Neither the master nor his assistants had ever worked on an assignment in such comfort. White gold, platinum, silver, lead, blue sapphires, garnets and rubies: Cox noted the gemstones, metals and other materials he required to realize his whims without ever justifying the quantities and passed the lists to Kiang to order— and they were sometimes delivered, amid much bowing, in a matter of hours and at the latest within a few days.

As if the most precious materials lay ready in inexhaustible piles for clockmakers and automaton-builders around the city, the English master's every last request was satisfied, and not once was he bothered by an enquiry as to the reason for his order. Although it was the Emperor's will that every wish be immediately fulfilled, the suppliers behaved as if the English master too had the power to conjure any jewel from nothing. Qiánlóng sent the Englishmen no greetings or messages and gave not the slightest indication of a visit.

This Emperor only wished to see finished works, Merlin guessed one radiant morning when the dust whisked into the air by the heat from the braziers described thermal spirals in the sunlight falling through the windows. Only finished works; no prototypes, no intermediate products, no operations.

Nothing, no work and no object, said Kiang, was to catch the Supreme Ruler's eye before it had been completed, because that eye ennobled and gilded. And gilding was reserved for what was complete.

Over the next few weeks, after several drafts had been rejected and revised, after many conversations in their workshop, the English guests started to build a white junk decked with waxed-silk sails.

Merlin, Lockwood and Bradshaw, all three of whom were accustomed to their master's extraordinary designs, had merely nodded when Cox had presented his plans. By late winter or next spring at the latest, this model of a junk, executed in white gold, platinum, sterling silver and brushed steel, boasting a pole mast and leeboards, was to become a *wind clock* that showed how time passed for a child: it would be a vessel surrounded by dancing waves of woven silver wire and lead, its metallic colours evoking shades of snow, ice, fog, cirrus clouds, down feathers, blank paper or innocence. An almost monochrome craft, no larger than a pillow including its rigging, and similar in construction to the barges Cox had seen gliding, almost floating, over the water during their journey on the rivers and lakes of China.

After all, few things had kindled Abigail's attention and excitement during her fleeting time on Earth more readily than the sight of sailing ships on the Thames, each with its attendant cloud of gulls.

They're showing them how! They're showing them how! Abigail had shouted jubilantly when she saw the flocks of gulls screeching and wheeling around a ship as they scavenged for fish waste. Abigail, his Abigail, had been sure that the birds were determined to demonstrate to the ships' crews how it was done: how to cruise along with sails beating like wings, gliding over the black water and then soaring into flight.

And this model's cargo would consist of gleaming baskets and tiny crates, sparkling packages, trunks and bundles. For did a child not expect or hope that every day would bring gifts? What riches, what surprises and wonders, produced by benevolent or menacing fairy-tale figures and spirits, might a single day or a single night of a child's life contain!

This age of surprises and wonders, and good, nasty or unsettling discoveries would be embodied by the cargo of a model ship that shimmered in every shade of white and silver. Following both the Western clock and Chinese timekeeping, which assigned different lengths to the hours of summer and winter, the packages, barrels and boxes would open by means of trapdoors and lids operated by filigree hinges and springs, revealing for an instant the sensations of the passing hours. These monochrome surroundings were illuminated by tiny, multicoloured sculptures of lacquered wood, bright gemstones, leather and rice-papier mâché—peacocks, dragons and trolls, revolving dancers and warriors, demons, fauns and angels, all connected by a complex mechanical system powered only by the rhythm of the wind, a draught or a puff of breath.

The sole source of energy for driving the mechanism hidden below decks to open and close the parcels, baskets and barrels were two silk sails and rig that could catch the gentlest air current and the slightest breeze in their waxed canvas, convert it into kinetic energy and transmit it via a shaft to the clockwork movement inside the junk. Should there be no breath of wind, no admirer to puff out his cheeks and fill the sail, the craft would stand still and so would time.

The alternation of immobility and leisurely or speedy progress would be dictated by nothing but the vagaries of draughts and gusts of wind; their varying tempos and strengths would recreate a child's sensation of time.

How quickly time passed when a child was expecting to be punished when its father got home, the hours flying by until he appeared in the doorway. (Cox recalled with astonishment that the Emperor himself had cited this example. Who could ever have punished this Almighty Ruler? Even his father, in deference to the timeless rules of his dynasty, would never have dared to lift a finger against an heir to the throne.) How slow, slow to the point of standstill, was the crawl of time during a school lesson, and how quick—at the speed of a falling stone—did a minute pass when a sweet melted on one's tongue . . .

These and similar comparisons were Cox's only words to his companions about the principle of a wind clock before he turned away and once more gazed out of the window into the court which lay empty and trackless.

Merlin smiled. A chaos-driven clock movement that looked like a child's toy: *this* was the master he knew from back home in England. *This* was the real Cox. And it was also slightly crazy, like virtually every automaton Cox had invented in the past, for this treasure would ultimately have to stand either out in the open air, where the breezy or gusty wind could reach it, or in the centre of a ring of servants and slaves, who would swell the junk's sails with their breath and thus offer a simultaneous reminder that a child not only had to be brought to life but also kept alive.

Although Bradshaw and Lockwood were pained during the first few weeks of work on the *silver ship* (as their master had authorized them to refer to the craft) by this contradiction of almost every tenet of their professional careers, since they had always previously aimed to convert the intervals by which time was measured into regular mechanical steps accurate to the second, they gradually began to take pleasure in the object that was taking shape and growing beneath their hands during those dull winter days. And it wasn't only Cox who thought of his daughter as he designed tiny porcelain mythical creatures, crowns and snakeheads dipped in lacquer to stow inside silver crates and baskets as part of the silver ship's cargo; his companions often forged long links, sometimes melancholic, often nostalgic, to their homeland, and they sawed, hammered and filed away as if preparing a surprise for the forthcoming Christmas festivities for which the Forbidden City knew no name.

Lockwood talked about his two sons, Samuel and David, who often fought over which of them was allowed to pull the rope that rang a local chapel's bells for evensong, only to snuggle up and sleep in the same bed later.

Bradshaw rhapsodized about his three daughters and their beguiling voices as, together, they sang songs by Tallis and Purcell, and about a gifted son who, at the age of only five, could walk a tightrope using a balance pole with an empty bucket dangling from each end—*dance* on it, Bradshaw said, dance.

Merlin was the only one who did not participate in these reminiscences. His wife Sarah had died during delivery, and Zoe, his only daughter, who had barely survived her birth, ceased growing before she learnt to read and write, as if her dead mother's love and strength had been only just sufficient to carry her through her first years in a sinister world. Zoe, a dwarf, now lived in hiding with Merlin's brother's family on a farm two days' ride from Manchester.

To the accompaniment of the work at the benches and to a hum of thoughts and memories that took him back to the quiet rooms of his house in Shoe Lane or to the halls of his manufactories, Cox kept returning in those first few weeks to the window from which he had watched the procession of litters and seen the blood-spluttering bearer die and . . . and the hand of that girl-woman which filled him with a mysterious longing.

Yet however much he yearned for the empty court stretching out before him to come to life, be it the spectacle of a courtly ceremony or a death, the court remained deserted and, when snow fell and more snow and further snow that no longer melted, it disappeared beneath a white vista which, as if in mockery of the monochrome nature of the silver ship, might, in the course of one wintry day, take on the colour of the impervious sky, the colour of the clouds and even of the steel-grey smoke wafting over the empty space from the beaked roofs of the pavilions and palaces like veils.

The English guests were attended by a constantly changing cast of silent servants and provided with everything they desired. Their living quarters and workplace were heated, the floors were swept and scrubbed every week with besoms and a lavender-scented soap solution, and their laundry washed with a regularity unheard of in England. Yet, despite their physical proximity to the seat of absolute power, life in the Purple City, governed by endless rules and laws, remained as incomprehensible and foreign as ever and occasionally menacing.

They were denied access to any place other than where they worked, ate and slept. They were invited to none of the festivals and ceremonies whose polyphonic sounds— bells, drums, bamboo flutes and strange wailing, shrill singing—drifted over the roofs and courts and walls and were even audible in their insulated living quarters, illu- minated by the spidery light of firework bouquets. They were escorted wherever they went by silent bodyguards selected from the ranks of the palace guard, and of all the things they heard or people called out or sometimes whispered to them at the market or in the streets, Kiang translated for his wards only that which laws beyond their ken permitted them to hear.

Even when they quit the often-deserted expanses of the palace district on their occasional expeditions into the heart of Běijīng, emerging into a vibrant maze of houses, narrow lanes and squares teeming with voices and faces, it was as if their escort created an impenetrable space around them, a bubble detached from the Emperor's inviolability, which encapsulated and allowed them to move freely but which no look, gesture or word could pierce.

Fuck, said Merlin; it was as if the life they led here condemned them to toil like the mechanical, clockwork figures of an automaton, driven by invisible cogs, like breathing embellishments to a machine controlled and piloted by engineers obeying the incomprehensible customs of a different planet.

What did you say? asked Bradshaw. Engineers? A different planet?

He's had too much rice wine, said Lockwood. It'll be Christmas soon. He's going on about planets. He's imagining things.

Fuck you, said Merlin.

Cox said nothing. As work continued and the silver ship became more visible and more tangible, his omnipotent patron seemed to recede ever further, as if he merely wished to test the English clockmakers' artistry, their ingenuity and technical skills and had now lost interest in both the progress and the results of their efforts.

Hadn't Abigail sometimes tired of her whirring ivory top? She would set it spinning with a gentle twist and then turn to a different toy; absorbed in the next game, she had forgotten all about the top by the time it toppled over or was chased by the cat into a dark corner and disappeared.

Kiang did not know either if the Emperor was following how work was progressing on the fog ship. After all, he was only authorized to present his report to a mandarin who noted what he had heard and passed the news on up the chain, where it was passed up and up, maybe archived and eventually forgotten.

How bothersome and even interfering the messengers of his aristocratic customers had been in London and Manchester by contrast; sometimes, the customers themselves would turn up at the workshops on a weekly and, in special cases, even a daily basis to check that Cox was not giving preferential treatment to an influential rival by prioritizing that man's order.

But here, silence. No enquiries. No messengers. No jealous visits. No visits whatsoever.

Neither Cox nor Kiang, whom the English guests began to mistrust and to privately suspect, despite his amiable diligence, of not being their friend but in reality a spy for the secret services, received any news or so much as a signal from the Emperor's entourage.

So the first message to reach their benches from the taboo areas of the Purple City—an alarming rumour— seemed to provide some explanation for his silence and indifference: the Almighty Ruler was on his sickbed and being treated, against the recommendations of his personal physicians, by Tibetan healers, by soot-smeared shamans whose incantations, rattles and bitter potions might turn an ailment into a ghoulish spectacle but could never alleviate, let alone cure it.

A rumour, said Kiang. Just a rumour from the Pavilion of Heavenly Tranquillity. Yet from the hesitant fashion and tone of voice in which Kiang uttered the word 'sickbed' and then stammered when he repeated it in answer to Merlin's concerned enquiry, Cox deduced that a more accurate translation would be 'deathbed'.

The Lord of Ten Thousand Years, the almighty Qiánlóng who wished to measure the many changes of pace in the course of a human life, from birth to the bier, from love nest to scaffold, had perhaps lost his power over the millennia to fever, perhaps to a plot, and would depart the world he governed in the coming days or even hours. Or maybe this instant, on his luxurious couch, and in the shadow of guards unable to hold him back or protect him any longer, he was fighting a losing battle against time.

7

LÍNG CHÍ

A Punishment

Just a rumour . . . It was indeed just a rumour—a lie!—
that the Unassailable One, the Invincible One was suffering from a fever or some other infirmity, even fighting
for his life.

The Master of Time, it said in a circular composed by
his mandarins and was read out to the long lines of assembled courtiers from the steps of the Pavilion of Terrestrial
Harmony before it was distributed and conveyed to the
English guests in Kiang's translation: the Lord of Ten
Thousand Years had developed an allergic reaction to fun-
gal spores from the Tibetan highlands which manifested
itself in pronounced lachrymation and stinging eyes. This
had prevented him from reading or composing documents

or any of the delightful poems he recited to grace the hours around daybreak. Two Tibetan healers had released the Lord of the Horizons from his troublesome yet harmless ailments in a single afternoon with the aid of a decoction of aloe berries, ground wild-rose seeds and rainwort—a potion whose formula would be nailed to the northern gate of the Purple City in the coming days for his people's benefit.

The Emperor was in rude health. He wrote, read, laughed and whispered or sang his poems into the quiet early hours, and his infallible judges had sentenced the instigators of the rumour, two jealous court physicians, to death. They had dared to question their supreme lord's decision to allow Tibetans to treat him for an ailment that originated in Tibet.

The interrogation of nine witnesses had established that the two doctors—one a surgeon, the other an eye specialist—had claimed at two conferences at least that the shamans from Lhasa would drum even an immortal into the tomb, that they would either blind or inflict other incurable harm on the Emperor with their murky concoctions and fetid extracts; yes, they had even claimed that the Supreme Ruler had allowed those barbarian quacks to deceive him. As if His Sublime Majesty could be tricked, fooled by fairground charlatans.

The court tribunal had deliberated for only three hours before reaching a verdict and a sentence: the day after the Great Snow Festival, the liars were to endure *ling chi—Creeping Death*. Shackled to posts and facing each other, one would be forced to follow the torture inflicted on the other, step by step, in the knowledge that it would be his own fate the next moment. The executioner would first use scissors to slice off their left nipple, then the right; next, he would hack through their chest with a knife, then the bunched muscles of the legs, starting on their thighs and continuing on their shanks, removing thin strips with each incision until the bones glinted through streams of blood. Next, the flesh of the upper and lower arms was to fall into the blood-soaked sawdust until the liars resembled dripping, screaming skeletons—reduced to ghosts not by the executioner but by their lies alone.

And only when each condemned men had witnessed the other's torments and then immediately suffered them himself, only when they had seen and suffered everything it was possible to see and suffer without dying . . . only then would their eyes be put out with an iron thorn dipped in hydrochloric acid, condemning the remains of their wretched lives to the blackest darkness.

At the end of a period defined by law and measured by the drips of a water clock, the executioner would sever the heads of the damned men from their torsos, not with a sword but with the same knife with which he had accomplished his work thus far, and impale each head on a spear. The spears were then to stand for twenty-one days and nights beside the towering fountain outside the gates of the stock exchange as a warning to all liars as well as to all bond traders who had already begun to speculate on a change of ruler, hoarding rice, tea and grain to drive up prices.

Surrounded by wheeling scavenging birds and buzzing flies that had emerged from hibernation, these skulls were to serve as a reminder to anyone conducting fraudulent deals at the stock exchange, banks and trading houses that his own head might well provide a perch for the next crow to sink its beak into an empty eye socket.

To prevent the condemned men's roars of pain from disturbing the serene peace of the Purple City under its snowy blanket, it was announced to the courtiers and the English guests, the punishment would be exacted far from the palaces on a notorious platform known as the Demon Barricade. Sacrificial fires and beacons were lit on it in turbulent times so that their flickering light would ward evil spirits and destructive phantoms away from the centre of the world.

The court and its entourage of officials, soldiers and aristocrats were advised to attend this performance of justice, even though screams of pain were hardly deemed a necessary reminder of their duty of absolute obedience and the excruciating consequences of any deviation: merely reading the verdict should suffice to warn anyone who lived in the direct vicinity of the seat of power about the Emperor's watchful and ubiquitous eye. Even the most piercing cries of pain faded to nothing with a condemned man's final heartbeats, but the text of the Emperor's verdict remained. Every letter penned by him was a revelation.

When this document, a wonder of calligraphy, reached the Englishmen's workshop and Kiang read it aloud, first, on his knees, in the original and only then in an English translation for the benefit of his bewildered listeners, it seemed that the already muffled sounds of their precision craftsmanship petered out, and it was clear that the reason for this abrupt decrease in the noise level, here as in every other corner of the Empire where the will and law of the Invincible One was pronounced, was terror.

From that time on, the junk's builders only mentioned the desperate plight of the two physicians when Kiang was elsewhere, and even then, without any prior collusion, in an indistinct and garbled dialect they assumed their translator would understand—if indeed he understood anything at all—only with a question mark over every word.

They butcher someone just because he can't hold his tongue? asked Lockwood.

Are the punishments for a loose tongue more lenient back home? asked Bradshaw. What if our lovely wind clock doesn't live up to expectations and the little silver ship runs aground? Shall we also find ourselves on stakes or dispatched to the butcher?

To whom else? said Merlin with a snigger. And our skulls will be turned into cuckoo clocks. Jumping jacks will spring from our eyes to mark the hours, and we'll spit stars of puffed rice at mealtimes and tinsel at midnight.

Be quiet, Jacob, said Cox. Be quiet.

The junk was coming on. From some of the silver baskets, crates and barrels in its cargo of toys, spirits brought to life by cogs were already rising, hammered-silver swallows and fantastic jade creatures were soaring upwards and the sails billowing with the rice-wine-soaked breath of Aram Lockwood, the hardest-drinking and sturdiest of the English guests, when Kiang entered the workshop with a message from His Sublime Majesty's Grand Secretariat:

Work on the wind clock was to be suspended. It was not to cease entirely, but to be deferred for a while in favour of a new clock movement.

Qiánlóng had not even seen the marvellous junk and its gearing, at least not with his own eyes, though Kiang's reports or those of another close observer among the guards must have kept him better informed than any ordinary visitor to the workshop could ever have been. Maybe Qiánlóng was acting on the recommendations of invisible advisers, his own intuition or merely clues that had come to him in a dream . . . For whatever reasons, the Lord of Ten Thousand Years suddenly seemed to be taking a more pressing interest in the daily and hourly rhythm of the end of a man's life than he did in the pace of childhood:

Cox was now to design and build a clock for the doomed and the dying, said Kiang, a chronometer for those condemned to death and all those who knew the date of their demise, saw the relentless approach of their life's final hour and could no longer soothe their nerves with hopes of the kind of elastic, provisional immortality with which most of the living deluded themselves about the finite nature of their existence.

For was even a terminally ill person not capable of deceiving himself, hoping for a miracle that would release him back into the world and thereby prolong his normal life? But once a judge empowered by the Emperor had sentenced a man to death, there could be no further doubts about his final hour to placate him. He saw the end and thus the future as unmistakably as only a god might otherwise.

Master Alister Cox, said Kiang, was to enjoy the privilege of collecting design material for his new work in death's antechamber, in the prison where the irresponsible doctors were now awaiting their executioners. He was authorized to talk to the two of them, listen to them, ask them about their lives and their guilt, and draw from these conversations the conclusions required to make a blue-print for a clock. He had been granted two three-hour visits to the dungeon near the Demon Barricade.

He did not require such visits, said Cox. After all, people in London were also hanged, beheaded, burnt and drowned and forced to endure the slow trickle of time until their final agony. He was familiar enough with the inexorable nature of the law to imagine the fleeting lifespan of a desperate man before the death sentence was carried out.

Cox had misunderstood something, said Kiang, and misunderstanding could prove dangerous at any stage of life. This visit was not a suggestion from His Sublime Majesty, no mere request; it was a statement of his will.

Two days before the beginning of the execution, scheduled for the small hours (which would allow the spectacle of mutilation to last into the evening, thereby demonstrating amid the fading light to the witnesses and onlookers gathered at the place of justice—demonstrating indeed to the heavens themselves—how one extinguished the final spark of a guilty man's life), Cox and Kiang were escorted to the jail near the Demon Barricade by four guards who trotted with a clatter alongside their litter.

In this crenelated building, resplendent with the crimson of the Forbidden City, there appeared to be a whole army of soldiers and guards but no prisoners other than the two condemned men. In the long corridor—dark despite the cold, sunny weather outside—leading to the windowless dungeon where the two men were chained to the stone walls, it was deathly silent.

In spite of the three torches, along with some incense sticks an obsequious jailor had lit against the stench, it took Cox a moment to tell the two chained men apart: the blood-, dirt- and vomit-encrusted face of the younger from the blood- and dirt-encrusted face of the other, much older man.

The younger man sobbed as the guard brightened the darkness with his torches, believing that Cox and Kiang and their company of guards were his executioners, come to drag him to the place of execution. The older stared in silence at the black straw on which he crouched.

The jailor propped two torches in holes in the stone floor, which were presumably for attaching chains when occupancy was higher, and said something to the prisoners in a surprisingly friendly tone, two or three short phrases that could only have meant that they would now be asked some questions that they were obliged to answer. Kiang didn't translate the jailor's words.

Cox was overcome with feelings of pity, disgust and outrage. Bring them some water, he said to the jailor. They need to wash their faces. I want to see their faces.

He felt as helpless as if the chains were fastened to his own ankles, and he was close to tears.

Kiang translated.

The jailor obeyed.

However, instead of washing themselves as they had been ordered, the prisoners drank from the bowls with the greed of people dying of thirst. When the jailor rebuked them, with an abrupt change of tone, and made to knock the bowl from the younger man's grasp, Cox said to Kiang more loudly than he had ever addressed him before: Tell that arsehole to let them be. Tell him to let them drink!

Kiang translated.

The jailor obeyed.

What neither of the men touched were the bowls of rice Cox ordered the jailor to bring. The younger reached out for one but he had to fight back his nausea at the mere idea of stuffing some rice into a mouth mangled by torture instruments or blows, and it took him a while to stifle the retching that shook his body.

What are your questions? Kiang leant against the open cell door in order to alleviate the smoke-tinged stench with a light draught. But Cox was thinking about the metallic lustre and the featherweight waxed-silk sails of the junk, Abigail's miniature ship, on which he would now have to suspend work—in favour of a clock that was to measure the last, harrowing chapter of a miserable life, and he said nothing. He had no questions.

You have to ask something, said Kiang.

But Cox had no questions.

So Kiang spoke to the condemned men and translated for Cox, sentence by sentence, what he wished to find out. Whether the days in this darkness, the final days of their lives, passed more quickly than those of their guilt-ridden past? Did time begin to speed up in this dungeon as they waited for the Emperor's sentence to be carried out? What was the pace of time down here?

And? said Cox, observing the prisoners' faces, the young one's more composed and cleaner now, the old man's as unchanging as if it were petrified. And? What did they say? Both of them had spoken.

The old man says that time no longer exists here, or, if it does, it stands still. And the young one says that the days race by without his feeling anything.

How can something race? said Kiang. How can something race, I asked him, without his feeling anything? And he said that it was like someone falling into a bottomless pit in a crate that has been nailed shut. He falls and falls without ever hitting the bottom and this lulls the man inside into the belief that there is no bottom, that there never was a bottom, never any falling, only this stinking, suffocating small space and the roar of rushing darkness.

The second of the two visits the Emperor had mandated, conducted the following day, a day when thick snow fell in watery flakes, making the long, echoing corridor to the dungeon seem even darker and more oppressive—for the jailor and the guards at least—followed much the same course as the first. Kiang and the Englishman asked questions, and the prisoners answered.

In fact, though, Cox did not ask any questions this time either but began, after Kiang had ended his long silence with a warning, to tell the two men in a form of soliloquy about his mute wife and his daughter, about the glittering Thames which sparkled despite all the refuse and the floating corpses, all the driftwood and rotting flotsam and all the shit that England's longest river carried past the walls and palaces of London, as if in mockery of, and as a memorial to, the stupidity of power; it sparkled in the light of the sun and the moon.

And he told them about the cruelty of the kings of England who had their relatives and loved ones stabbed or beheaded, about the barbaric vanity of the high aristocracy who believed they were floating in the shimmering heights when they were actually trudging through sewage . . . stories, on and on, told as protest against the will of an emperor who was trying to order him—order him!— to ask questions.

He, Alister Cox, refused to ask these unfortunate men any questions or to use their answers for a clock design.

Never. Clocks and automata were bright, glittering allegories and premonitions of eternity, not means of measuring despair or absurd musical boxes of death.

Kiang, who was the only one who understood that Cox was putting his life on the line, did not translate a word of these tales; instead, whenever Cox paused, he asked the prisoners questions that matched Cox's tidings of England in both length and intonation. Kiang asked them about the duration of their sleepless hours, about the endlessness of a night spent awake in their chains, about the speed with which their erstwhile life of honour and dignity they had forfeited by the death sentence retreated ever further out of reach until it vanished completely.

The prisoners began to whisper after some of his questions, even lapsing into bland monologues which Kiang cut off but of which he translated not a single word, putting his own words in their mouths so as not to breach the visit's stipulated succession of questions and answers. For in fact the doomed men were no more providing answers than Cox was asking questions. They stammered requests for mercy and, encouraged by the gifts of rice and water that Cox had demanded and the jailor reluctantly brought, begged for bandages for the wounds sustained under torture and for help for their families, deprived of a breadwinner now.

After a while the elder was simply whispering names— no words, no sentences, only names that Kiang realized were the names of his loved ones: his wife, his children and the names of benevolent spirits to see him through his day of anguish. Cox did not understand a word.

On this stinking day, in this place lit exclusively by torches despite the sun shining high above, a day when the date and hour of their death was fixed as firmly as an astrologer's calculations of a celestial event, when there was no longer any hope of even the tiniest reprieve, all of mankind—whether in chains like the condemned men, in gleaming armour like the guardsmen or dressed in fine cloth like Kiang and the Englishman—seemed utterly abandoned, and everyone, whatever he might say or believe he understood, was alone.

WÀN LI CHÁNG CHÉNG

The Wall

On the day of the two court physicians' execution, a peaceful silence lay over the Forbidden City. No beat of the gong, no sound of the torment reached the Immortal One's residence, not one of the thousands of voices raised by the immense crowd swarming around the scaffold in the freezing cold, greeting each of the executioner's gestures with a chorus of lingering groans and occasionally with a rousing cheer and even laughter. No matter what was happening on the scaffold or in the throng of spectators, above whose craning necks the bloody platform seemed to float and even drift like a raft on the deep, the Hall of Supreme Harmony, the Palace of Terrestrial Tranquillity and the other seats of imperial power remained enveloped in cold silence, broken only occasionally by the call of a bird.

And as if the slow death of the condemned doubters of the Emperor's immortality and the barely imaginable agonies they endured on the scaffold through morning, midday and afternoon were just a harmless performance, at noon it began to snow.

The snow swirled along the empty processional avenues of the Purple City and over deserted squares reserved for the highest dignitaries, replacing recently dislodged or thawed pads on wall tops and in the twigs of ancient umbrella pines, renewing the white camouflage on guards' helmets and armour, levelling out the relief of rows of golden tiles on the roofs of the pagodas and transforming the blooms of the last roses—which gardeners had wrapped in silk shrouds against the frost—into faceless, crystalline heads.

In the afternoon, the rising wind gathered the whirling flakes into long, tattered banners that fluttered silently over the roof ridges and frozen gargoyles, and smothered all colour and form, as if the snow were seeking to blanket not only the execution site but also every nook and cranny and lane of a city that was violating the laws of compassion.

Many voluntary spectators at the execution, even certain mandarins and official observers, had chosen not to go to bed the previous night, after the fireworks and exuberant dancing of the Great Snow Festival celebrations. Instead, they had set out in the early hours from their revelries all over Běijīng to the execution site so that there, still intoxicated and dazzled by the glare of countless showers of sparks and veils of light raining down from the night sky, they might witness a horrifying alternative outcome to festivities and fun—an ending that plunged them into the darkness of death.

Escape? said Bradshaw shortly before lunch in the blizzard-dimmed workshop. Shouldn't we escape before they chain us to stakes too, cut us into strips and stick iron thorns into our eyes because, according to some sycophantic courtier, our clocks don't keep the right time?

Escape to where? said Lockwood. Through the dark and the fog and the fields to Shànghǎi? Disguise ourselves as ladies-in-waiting and hide in a litter till the next checkpoint, or sail down the Grand Canal on our silver ship?

Nostalgic for the courts of London, are we, Balder? asked Merlin. Do you prefer the crows pecking at a man swinging from the gallows above the Thames to the scavengers of Běijīng? Wasn't one of your cousins strung up for mutiny? And here? Here, eunuchs and armed warriors bow down before you. Here, you have servants to polish your shoes, starch your shirts, heat your workshop and your bedroom and place hot stones under your sheets to keep the goosebumps at bay!

Cox's companions chatted more loudly than usual that silent, snowy day, but Kiang did not hear a word. He had been dispatched to the execution site—he would not reveal if the order had come from his own department or some higher authority—so that he might subsequently report to the Englishmen on the mercilessness with which anyone who disturbed the Emperor's peace was banished not only from the greatest, most magnificent city on the globe but from the world itself.

The midwinter weeks passed without Qiánlòng's empire paying any heed to the birth of a god in a dusty, holy land or the dawn of a new year in an insignificant, grey nowhere. With Kiang's assistance Merlin attempted to teach the guesthouse cooks the recipe for plum pudding, but to no avail. None of the cooks could believe that the described procedure might produce an edible result. Instead, they offered the Englishmen meringues made from lychees, ground dried mangoes and the beaten whites of quails' eggs.

Cox began drawing up plans for a clock that would fulfil the Emperor's wishes and display and measure the cruising, racing or congealing passage of time over the final stages, days and hours of a man's life.

My word, this thing looks like a Christmas scene outside the walls of Bethlehem, like a crèche, said Bradshaw, when Cox showed his companions the first charcoal sketch of the clock case. All that was missing were the star, the shepherds and the three wise men from the East.

That isn't Bethlehem, said Merlin. It's Qiánlóng's Great Wall—the Great Wall of China.

The outline showed the model of a section, including five beacon towers, of the defensive wall that was almost five thousand nautical miles long, connecting mountains, deserts, lakes and other natural barriers, and had been enhanced by ruling dynasties over the centuries to encompass the shrinking, then expanding boundaries of their empire and protect their dominion from the onslaught of barbarian hordes.

To the eyes of its first critical beholder, Kiang, the model of the Great Wall—which was to become the precious case of the new clock, whose details, walkways, crenelations and machicolations became clearer in Cox's drawings with every passing day—was not merely a fragmentary representation of the greatest structure in human history, which the English guests had only seen in pictures and watercolours and on tapestries. A suspicious official might well interpret this clock case, said Kiang, as a mockery of the Great Wall—and that would attract punishment.

Wàn li cháng cheng—the Unimaginably Long Wall, Kiang called the Emperor's structure, for Wàn li did not just mean ten thousand *li*; *li* also stood for infinity. A ten-thousand-*li*-long wall was therefore ten thousand times unimaginably long.

This wall had been extended in all directions under the dynasties of the Qín and the Hàn, the Wèi, the Zhōu, the Táng, the Liáo and the Míng, without coming to an end. The *Great Dragon*, the name by which the wall had insinuated itself into the minds of the people, raised vaporous plumes and gigantic clouds with its fiery tongue from the waters of the Yellow Sea, while whipping up sand storms thousands of miles away among the dunes of the Gobi Desert with its tail . . .

And now a red-gold model of this wonder of the world, said Kiang, was to encase the mechanism of a clock that measured not the boundless scope of the Emperor's might, which this towering wall was designed to perpetuate, but, rather, the course of the disappearing, evaporating time that remained for a condemned or dying man to live? A desperate man, who did not rule this world but was on the point of departing from it for ever.

How great a step, asked Kiang, was it then from this interpretation to an accusation that the English guests' ticking clock sought to deride this wall! A toy made of a substance which, to top everything, glowed in a colour befitting no one but the Emperor?

That's your interpretation, said Merlin, and it's slanderous. A smarter man than our esteemed translator ought to have no trouble recognizing that Master Cox was building this piece to pay homage to his host. As for the golden colour, was this clock not intended for the Emperor? In which case, was there any more fitting tribute than lustrous gold, even if it marked time for a man who was dying or condemned to death?

To his companions' astonishment, after executing the construction plans in ink and then copying them by his own hand, Cox did not send them to their workbenches in early February so that they might measure, saw and sand the precious materials needed to build a Chinese wall reduced to the size of a table clock. No, instead he instructed them to grind ginger, cloves and powdered galangal in porcelain dishes; cardamom, red sandalwood, saffron, star anise, lavender and curls of cedar wood, rose resin and further spices, which Kiang delivered in linen bags and veneered wooden cases labelled by calligraphers; plants for which there were no English names, dried or compacted into grotesque shapes.

Are we precision mechanics or apothecaries? asked Bradshaw, trying to adopt a cheerful tone. Herb-gatherers or automaton-builders?

Without our assignment we are nothing in this city or this land, said Cox. Herbs reduced to ash were to be the heart and the soul of the new clockwork movement, the slag from embers eating their way inexorably through the final hours of a man's life, transforming all matter and even time itself to dust.

The characters with which Kiang titled a report informing his department of the English master's latest progress emphasized the result that would spiral up from the battlements and watchtowers of the miniature wall: *xunkao* and *yànyún* and *méiyan*—smoke, coal smoke, clouds of smoke . . . The master from England wished to build a fire clock whose mechanism would consume time.

First, though—and for as long as it took him to calculate the materials for his Great Wall and draw up lists of every troy ounce of gold, every ruby and brilliant to be inserted in this piece that would splinter daylight and candlelight into a hundred shards and make them sparkle in the eye of the beholder—Cox wanted his companions to reproduce, following ancient recipes, the incense that veiled entire palaces with blue clouds on certain days. They were to knead the pounded herbs, gum Arabic and ground charcoal of tropical wood into pellets and spheres of every conceivable size.

This fuel was to fall in varying densities through funnels concealed inside the clock and roll down the various slopes and walkways atop the wall into white-hot pans where it would be reduced to the ash that would ultimately drive this clock while also releasing an extraordinary variety of aromas, ranging from the stench of old age and the odour of anxious perspiration to flower fragrances and the many scents of memory.

There would be five pans to match the number of watch-towers, and the ash would fall through holes in the bases of the pans onto precision scales sensitive to the weight of a single hair, thus tipping the scales, which were connected to drive shafts, to provide the decisive impetus to one of the larger or smaller cogs in the movement.

Depending on the speed—sometimes racing, sometimes crawling—of the burning process, which underpinned the production of ash, smoke and all the scented, stale or stinging aromas, the clock would change speed in unpredictable fashion, slow one moment, faster the next, occasionally even stopping for a few moments while the smoke from the watchtowers shrouded its hourly cycles in white fog . . .

For a man on his deathbed, said Cox—this was one morning when the light and warmth suggested that the end of winter was nigh, when a blackbird could be heard singing in the court outside the workshop—; for a man waiting for his executioner or confronting his mortal fear on a battlefield or in the depths of the desert, far from any succour; for such a man, time no longer followed any course but leapt and plunged from one level to another, soaring and plummeting and gliding so that a clock's second hand became its hour hand, and twenty or one hundred breaths later he had the feeling that whole days and weeks had passed in the time it took for the hour hand to move—or all the clock hands suddenly froze in an inkling of eternity.

That's your idea for a clock? asked Bradshaw.

Another toy, said Lockwood.

And what difference is there, Merlin asked, between a clock driven by trickling ash and our silver ship powered by breath and the wind? What's the difference between a glittering children's clock and this red-gold deathly smoke-maker for the condemned?

The same difference there is between any two clocks, said Cox. The difference in the beholder, in the person seeking to read time and his remaining years from it.

Then we might as well sail our silver ship through the cell of a man condemned to death or through the fug of a death chamber, and place this little golden wall beside a newborn's cradle, said Merlin. The dials of automata such as these displayed the course of time to a dying man in the same way they showed it to a newborn whose life had only just begun.

Both mothers *and* their babies can die in childbed, said Cox. Whatever we build—a clock movement, a machine—reveals the contents of our own heads, at best its owner's wishes or those of a client.

Is that all there is to it? asked Merlin.

That is all, said Cox.

While Cox was describing his plans in detail to Kiang the next day, so that their translator and intermediary could pass on quantities and lists to his department and their suppliers, the companions occasionally had the impression that Kiang was not noting down the materials they required but merely the thoughts that came to his mind as he listened to Cox. He seemed to be listening as if he were not involved, making brushstrokes on the paper that bore no recognizable relation to what Cox was telling him about how the ember clock worked. His face merely took on an attentive look, then a horrified expression when Cox stated that he wished to travel as soon as possible with Merlin to the Great Wall near Jīnshānlǐng so that he might finally see for himself this rampart built to withstand time itself and sketch it before determining the final dimensions and form of the ember clock.

That section of the wall runs through the Yānshān mountains which is a military exclusion zone, said Kiang.

Am I a spy? asked Cox.

Anyone who sees things not intended for his eyes is a spy, said Kiang, for at some unguarded moment, inadvertently, he's bound to mention what he has heard or seen to unauthorized individuals.

A spy, said Cox. And what does one call a man who is trying to stop me from doing the Emperor's bidding? My work demands that I study the Great Wall. After all, the clock had to be an exact likeness of the section of the wall standing on the silk carpet in the guesthouse tearoom—the section between Sīmǎtái and Jīnshānlǐng, as Kiang himself had remarked some weeks earlier about the model on the carpet. That part of the wall crawled up steep slopes towards mountain ridges and peaks, and then just as steeply back down from the heights, and frequently out of the clouds into a dark-green, rocky wilderness.

After Cox's demand, Kiang was not seen in the workshop for two days. When he knocked on the door around noon on the third day with nothing but a light pack and six horsemen armed to the teeth, Cox thought they had come to arrest him.

Labouring under their burden of spears, bows, shell-encrusted leather quivers bursting with arrows, daggers, swords and bulky muskets whose butts were inlaid with tortoiseshell, the horsemen looked more like warriors heading into battle than guardsmen constituting the Englishmen's daily escort. (An archer, Merlin was to be told a few hours later by one of these riders, was faster and more lethal in a skirmish than a musketeer who had to drive the gunpowder and ramrod into the muzzle-loading gun while holding the lead ball in his mouth before spitting the latter into the barrel and firing it. However, the terror unleashed by a shot fired at point-blank range and the horror at the wound a lead ball could inflict on an enemy's chest and head were greater than the impact of a silent, deadly arrow.)

Flanked by these mute warriors, Kiang announced in fairly solemn tones that the master's request would be fulfilled. Here—for Merlin and Cox, he had brought horses, saddled and draped with furs. Bradshaw and Lockwood were to stay in the city and wait at their workbenches for the others to return.

No, there were no carriage tracks through the wet spring snow of the forests along the wall near Jīnshānlǐng, nothing but the bridle paths of the border patrols. So they would have to ride the seventy or eighty miles into the Yānshān mountains. It was likely to take four or five days to explore the Great Wall, depending on how long and from how many different angles Cox wished to survey the wonders of a structure that reached back so deep into the past and stretched so far into the future. In the meantime, the companions who had remained behind were to fashion pellets according to Cox's instructions—hundreds and hundreds of spheres of all sizes—from the spice dough, carefully wrapped in oilcloth, and produce many decades' worth of fuel for a clock that measured life going up in smoke.

There was no time for any further preparations. Cox had wished to see the Great Dragon with his own eyes as a model for his automaton, and the court had approved this plan. They must therefore set off. Now. Whatever someone requested at the court of His Sublime Majesty, if it was granted, its granting transformed the wish into an order, and that order was to be immediately executed.

Within the hour, nine riders passed through the north gate of the Forbidden City into the labyrinthine lanes of Běijīng and out into the snowbound countryside. Cox noticed none of the many eyes following their departure from behind curtains and shutters. He had last ridden many years ago and had trouble recalling the correct posture to spare one's spine and pelvis during days in the saddle. The animal kept floundering in wind-compacted snowdrifts and would gladly have thrown the rider imperilling its balance.

Merlin didn't fare much better. Aren't there any roads around here? he asked Kiang.

This is the road, Kiang said.

The ride gave them no leisure to savour the lingering views over the white landscape, dotted with creaking bamboo groves waving their snowy plumes, or glimpses of low hills and scattered farms and hamlets. They crossed paths with a dispatch rider leading a steaming spare horse; mistaking the two foreigners with their escort of six warriors and a masked civilian for prisoners, he enquired about their crime. Although Cox and Merlin were wrapped in fur coats and blankets and wearing leather masks against the fierce wind, their size and uncertain posture gave them away as *cháng bizi*—long-noses. Perhaps they had been caught trespassing in forbidden territory.

Their crime? an archer answered with a grin. Stupidity. Stupidity was their only crime. They wanted to ride through the deep snow to the Great Wall instead of sitting by the fire over some soup and a cup of wine.

What did he say? asked Merlin.

Nothing, said Kiang. A greeting.

By late afternoon they had covered barely a third of the distance to the first sight of the Wall. A charcoal-burner chopping wood for the winter in a pine plantation made a vain attempt to flee when he saw the armed horsemen approaching through the thickening dusk, but after a few calming words from Kiang he reluctantly offered them a billet in his house while he and his seven-strong family moved into a soot-streaked storeroom for the night.

When the horseman who had used his lasso to prevent the charcoal-burner from fleeing then forced the man, once he had unsaddled the horses, to take repeated swigs from a leather flask of rice liquor, he put a brave face on these frightening circumstances and began to sing in a high-pitched voice. Yet the next morning, after a wordless farewell, he fell weeping, his arms raised, to his knees in the snow, for one of the archers pretended to kidnap their host's adolescent daughter, heaving the girl into the saddle beside him as she was handing him a bread-bag, and racing off in a shower of snow.

When the troop caught up with him a short time later, he released the trembling and distraught girl with a laugh, and she traipsed back towards her father's house through the deep, wet snow, first in her clogs but then, after the first few paces, in her stockings.

Kiang did not comment on any of this. Cox too had been fooled by the warrior's crude prank, imagining Abigail, his deceased little girl, draped across the horse-man's saddle. He had cried out in protest but had been incapable of articulating his indignation in any words or threats the kidnapper might have understood or seen as sufficient motivation to do, or not do, something . . . and yes, despite the sudden, stabbing memory of Abigail, he had been too craven, too weak to stay the ruffian's arm.

But why, for hell's sake, had Kiang not intervened? Why had he looked on in silence?

Not to fear these warriors, said Kiang, is to misunderstand their nature.

Around noon the next day, after a cold night in the two tents carried by packhorses, the Great Dragon appeared so suddenly between ridges, crags and peaks surrounded by a tide of high-altitude forests groaning under the weight of snow, that Cox only noticed the miraculous sight when Merlin called it to his attention. They had scrambled their way across a scree slope and come to a hilltop with a scattering of pines and mulberry trees when the Emperor's wall appeared, complete with battlements and beacon towers, like a garland that had been carried away by the wind and snagged on peaks and ridges.

The wall divided empty, unpopulated mountains from more empty, unpopulated mountains, running almost gracefully, daintily even, in a narrow vanishing line towards a hazy horizon, changing course along a ridge before once more swinging back after an umpteenth bend onto the ideal line imagined by long-forgotten architects and generals, trailing behind it a chain of towers which shrank from menacing fortifications to faint dots.

None of the riders had given the signal to halt, but they all stopped as if on command, spellbound by the sight of this rampart nestling in apparently uncharted, untouched wilderness which had not once been overrun in the course of many centuries.

That is . . . Merlin said, beginning a sentence that he broke off after a few syllables, abandoning a futile attempt to describe the emotions this gigantic monument in the middle of a deserted, dripping winter landscape triggered inside him. Birdsong had begun to mingle with the whisper and gurgle of meltwater. Like the wall, their singing seemed to sheer off into boundless realms, as if the thousand-voice song with which the birds wooed, defended their territory or warned off attackers were the sound and the voice of the wall itself, stretching as far into the distance as the receding series of towers and battlements.

It was strange that after so much effort and movement, interrupted only by two short, virtually sleepless nights, their halt on this hilltop and this silent view seemed all of a sudden to have become their journey's goal. A border guard or wood gatherer, spotting the nine horsemen and their packhorses from afar, might have mistaken this troop for a monument, a memorial to a battle on the border or a statue in honour of victorious or fallen defenders of the empire. None of the warriors dismounted. Despite their aching backs, Cox and Merlin still preferred their fur-covered saddles to the sodden forest floor where they would first have had to establish a dry campsite.

One arm outstretched, Kiang pointed eastwards and said, Jīnshānlǐng, then westwards with his left arm: Sīmǎtái. They had arrived.

Somewhere along this line of countless watchtowers straddling hills, ridges and summits must be the group of five fortresses on which the gold case for the Emperor's clock was to be modelled.

Which way now? Down into the valley and from there up to the next hilltop, almost indistinguishable from this one, and so forth?

Before Cox could decide or even weigh up whether he really should seek out those five towers and allow them to fire his imagination like a landscape painter, make the most of his privileged status and set foot on top of the wall, or content himself instead with this grand view, one of the soldiers' horses, a piebald gelding, reared whinnying onto its hind legs, and the horseman, lost in contemplation of the vast expanses before him or maybe enjoying a snooze, was unable to catch hold quickly enough and fell with a clatter into the snow.

The fact that all the weapons the man wore and bore, along with his shield, his helmet and his breastplate, were unable to prevent him falling off his horse after its sudden lurch struck Cox as such an odd interruption of his peaceful reverie that he only just managed to stifle a convulsive fit of laughter. He disguised the sound that burst forth from his mouth as a cough and cleared his throat. It was only then that he saw the arrow shaft: the projectile, as shiny as if it were lacquered, and fletched with feathers, was embedded deep in the horse's neck, and blood was already spurting from around it.

What followed this attack seemed as automatic as the whirring cogs of a mechanized process. With the agility and speed of a wind-whipped swirl of fallen leaves and a few quiet commands, the horsemen formed a tight circle around their three wards and their fallen comrade; he leapt onto a packhorse despite his armour and heavy weapons and had already nocked an arrow to his bowstring by the time he landed in the saddle. One man, whom the others had referred to during simply as *Kĕ, the Thirsty One*, the only name Cox could remember due to its brevity, now revealed himself to be the troop's commander, gesturing to his three wards to flatten themselves over their mounts' withers so as not to offer targets for further arrows.

The wounded horse was forced out of the ring, no more than a snorting shield now, bucking and throwing back its head to dislodge the painful incisor, tusk or beak planted in its neck, dancing around the circle of horsemen like a will-o'-the-wisp and perhaps interfering with the aim of a second archer or spear-thrower lurking in the undergrowth.

The snorting of the panicking, injured animal was the only sound. No cry, no roar came from the invisible enemy, no word either from the defenders whose readied arrows and spears jutted out in every direction from their close-drawn circle, but there was nothing but black trees clad in a dripping armour of snow on all sides. There were no enemy tracks on the forest floor around them.

Huddled low over his pommel, Cox could see nothing but a hand's breadth of his fur blanket. Even after one, then two long minutes, he still did not dare to raise his head, saw nothing, heard nothing from Merlin, no sound from Kiang and his protectors, saw only this skin, wondering all of a sudden which animal it might once have kept warm, and when and in what conditions this animal had been killed—on a hunt? at a slaughterhouse?—and catching whiffs of grease and smoke and wet wool, and he began to shrink into that hairy moss-like pelt, into a large and comforting nest, a woollen refuge in which he could hide and make himself invisible, a refuge so soft and enveloping and yielding that it was impossible to breach, making invulnerable anyone who gave himself into its protection.

It had been as warm and safe and yet unsettling as this in his mother's arms when she picked him up and rocked him, and he buried his head in one of the fur stoles with which, until the hour of her death, she had shielded her nape from draughts. A single breath of cold air brushing her neck might plunge her into days of pain during which a pounding migraine could confine her to a room darkened by black blinds. During that time, even a single ray of light would pierce her like a needle or a knife.

Only her son's warm breath, a hint of which permeated her fur stole, could alleviate that pain, and the weight of her child, who sometimes wept at his mother's mysterious torments, would eventually seem so light that she felt as if his body had become one with hers, or as if she had only just conceived this creature that shared her suffering.

Hunched over his horse's withers, Cox slid into his memories while his breath, reflected back at him by the fur, warmed his face. Warmed it. Shouldn't he feel cold, as he usually did when scared by something from his earliest childhood?

He did not shiver. He was lying, weary but content, against his mother's fur-protected neck when he felt Merlin's hand on his shoulder and raised his face from the skin. It was the tanned coat of a Bactrian camel.

How long had it been since he had last taken refuge in his mother's arms?

Merlin and Kiang were sitting upright in their saddles, surrounded by angry warriors peering and pointing their arrows in all directions, and two brandishing muskets. Cox sat up too, a lingering odour of pelt in his nostrils.

Nothing had happened. Nothing more. And nothing more happened. One arrow: that was all. The archer who had turned his weapon on the Emperor's warriors had stayed out of sight and belonged either to a horde so superior in numbers that they could rebel against the builder of an infinitely long wall—or was so alone in his rage and powerlessness that all he could do was make a gesture, a ridiculous sign, and his sole triumph was to attract the attention of imperial soldiers for a few seconds, thereby proving that meekness and obsequious obedience were not the only response to the servants of an immortal.

Of course, brigands probably showed equal disregard for the law, but here, spying heavily armed warriors, they had protested with an arrow against their own inferiority and possibly in frustrated anticipation of easy pickings. Well, maybe the arrow had merely been a poor shot by a hunter, a starving woodsman now crouching somewhere in the bushes, paralysed by fear, hoping that these raging men wouldn't find him and avenge his calamitous miss with the only punishment such an attack merited—excruciating death.

As the ring of horses gradually began to loosen and, pursued by questions of this kind, eventually to disperse, one thing at least was clear: that there could be no further observation of the Great Wall that would match the serenity and profundity of their rapt, quiet contemplation before the ambush. From now on, any viewing would be marred by a state of extreme vigilance and alertness, and could therefore not provide Cox with a model for the case of his ember clock to surpass the tapestry that had inspired his drawings.

In any event, Kě, now the troop's undisputed commander, entertained no further considerations. After all, whatever else the English guests might wish to see on this idiotic venture, his principal duty was to return them to the Purple City unscathed. If he were to imperil their lives, his own life would be in danger, even if he were to be the sole survivor of the next attack. This fir-plumed hilltop, from which the Great Dragon could be admired in its full insurmountable splendour, would be their turning point.

From here, Kě decided without consulting Kiang, all roads led back to the safety of the Purple City.

When the fallen warrior put the wounded gelding's saddle on one of the packhorses, tightened its blood-soaked girth and made to deliver the *coup de grâce* to the attack's only victim, exhausted from its desperate bucking, Kě shook his head. And so the saddleless, bridleless gelding trotted along behind the horsemen for a while as they rode downhill, repeatedly tumbling to the ground from weakness caused by its loss of blood, struggling back to its feet and lagging ever further behind until after a time it disappeared behind a crag.

Kiang tried to translate for the Englishmen the six warriors' speculations about the source of the single arrow until he realized that neither Merlin nor Cox showed any particular interest in what he was saying. In his thoughts Cox was still beside the Great Wall and was likely to gaze up at it for a long time yet. A single arrow had sufficed to beat back a troop of imperial horsemen, and this in the shadow of a wall designed to defend the progress and prosperity of an imperial civilization from the onslaughts of domestic and foreign barbarians, transforming its unimaginable length into an endless trail of ashes that seasonal gusts scattered in clouds of grey flakes.

9

ĀN

The Beloved

Though humiliated by a single arrow, the riders were accompanied on their journey back into the centre of the empire by a constant, tangy spring wind as if, despite their disgrace, they were returning with precious spoils from their expedition to the Great Wall. The closer they came to their destination, the air along their route, which led less and less frequently over tongues of snow, then only over boggy ground and pale wintry meadows, was redolent with the incomparable fragrances, sounds and voices of spring.

Even in the lanes on the outskirts of Běijīng, where meltwater flushed faeces and stinking waste from the gutters, the scent of moist moss, woodland soil and rain-polished rocks drifted over the pungent stench. *Turdus mandarinus*, the Chinese blackbird, whose silhouette Cox knew from an index of bird models for musical boxes, seemed so carried away in its enthusiasm for the end of winter that it imitated a full repertoire of the everyday sounds issuing from open windows—the crying of an infant, the singing of a tea kettle or the sighing scales of a bamboo flute that a nameless pupil was desperately repeating on pain of being beaten with his teacher's cane . . . Scraps of smoke rising from sacrificial temple bowls drew a merciful veil over the black mould, damp marks and pox-like patches of rotten roughcast on the houses of subjects not fortunate enough to bask in the light and warmth of the court's splendour.

When the troop reached the gardens surrounding the master's companions' guesthouse, the horses trampled into the damp, black earth dozens of seedlings just unfurling their first tiny leaves, but the vigour of life thrusting into the sunlight was so great that even the warhorses' hoofmarks in the flowerbeds were little more than helpless reminders of the power of destruction, no more threatening than a single arrow fired at the endless lengths of the Great Wall.

Without entering the gates, the horsemen handed over their wards to four disinterested guards and vanished as silently and suddenly as they had appeared outside the master's residence a few days earlier, in what now seemed a bygone season.

Bradshaw and Lockwood had emerged from the house, greeting them with two bowls in which freshly rolled, glowing incense balls released cavorting whorls and aromas of lavender and hyacinth, and casting admiring glances after the riders as they trotted away, seemingly melded to their horses, breastplates and shields. Sprays of feathers in the blood-like colours of the Purple City blazed on their helmets, and from their saddlecloths, trimmed with strips of tiger skin, dangled thumb-sized drops of amber inside which insects encased millions of years ago had outlasted time—water spiders, lacewings and even scorpions, startled and trapped by a slow-moving trickle of resin, liberating them in similar fashion, perhaps, to the Lord of Ten Thousand Years from the all-consuming course of time.

Carved garnet flames sparkled on the reins and bridles of the departing warriors as a sign that the lord in whose name they cut their way through gardens or battlefields ruled not only over time but also over fire and the light of the sun and the stars which tempted from the darkness, gently, cautiously and irresistibly, the hidden life of countless colours and forms slumbering deep in the soil.

Why don't we use one of these warriors as a model and build a musical clock in his image? said Bradshaw. A heroic figurine that bows before the seasons, gauges the strength of the winds with its feathers and strikes the hours with its sword and shield?

Warriors do not live long enough to serve as proper time-keepers, and a waving crest trampled into the mud by a warhorse's hooves does not even twitch in a hurricane, said Merlin, as a eunuch on all fours wiped the dirt from his boots with his greasy brown tunic.

Over the next few radiant spring days, Cox left the golden watchtowers, the walls, the entire case of his ember clock as it was, not undertaking even the slightest alteration, as if he had pre-empted the sight of the real thing with his design and had only been verifying during the ride to the Great Wall that his plans reflected every detail of the real thing. But while Lockwood and Bradshaw were at last allowed to cease producing the aromatic fuel for this clock and once more devote themselves, along with Merlin, to its mechanisms, the master appeared to have lost interest.

Well, the technical aspects had been solved, the construction plans, laid out in China ink, lay ready for their transformation into precision instruments, and Cox still gave instructions every morning, checking, correcting and praising—but he would always withdraw for the rest of the day into a dingy corner of the workshop behind a nine-panelled cherrywood screen painted with bamboo leaves. There, the silver junk, capable of sailing through time and a child's immortal life, draped with lengths of silk to protect it from dust and draughts, awaited His

Majesty's inspection, awaited the Emperor's admiring or disappointed gaze. And behind that screen, hidden in a flurry of painted leaves that an anonymous court artist had reproduced with such verve that Merlin claimed he could hear the wind whispering in the foliage, Cox began to make corrections and additions without the aid of his companions.

He rebuilt the barrel and replaced the lever escapement and regulator with components of such accuracy that the aim now seemed to be to build an astronomical chronograph; he even mounted an additional transmission gearing for a second movement concealed below the deck and, lastly, cut tuned teeth and cylinders for a musical box to play the tunes of three children's songs about the sun (Cox knew no others).

Never before in the history of automata and timepieces had such a musical machine been built. Even his companions raised their heads in astonishment when they heard the master humming behind his painted foliage, followed by sequences of metallic notes in the same key as the melody Cox had just sung.

In its creator's mind, the junk, transformed into a toy for Abigail, was to have a voice and a second movement in its hold, driven not by the wind in the sails but wound by the fine chain attached to an anchor glittering against the ship's hull and which measured a very different tempo from a child's—the hours, days and years of its designer and builder.

This secret mechanism would attune Cox's own time to that of his child for at least as long as a beholder's puff or a simple draught filled the junk's sail. Hadn't that which he had once regarded as the very essence of his life and joy come to a halt when his daughter died and his wife fell silent, like a clock whose power reserve was exhausted?

Just as the clock beneath the deck could be re-activated with a tug on the anchor, so too Cox only awoke each day to a better life when a thought of Abigail or Faye brushed him, saturated him—and enabled him to mechanically pursue an undertaking, a plan or an imperial order, and continue, hour after hour, to breathe, speak, be silent . . .

Yet everything in him stood still, again and again, every time the unrequited pining for his loved ones plunged him into a state of empty sorrow, in which he was no longer able to think or recall but only to fall into exhausted sleep, so that, both paralysed and persecuted by incoherent dreams, he could embark on a futile quest for the theatres of his memories.

Upon awakening, a first thought of their faces, of Abigail's eyes, laughter or tears would move him to set his clock in motion by taking the tiny, glittering anchor between his thumb and forefinger, pulling the chain taut and, after a deep breath, filling the sails of the junk with his sighs. Now both movements ran in harmony, not in sync but in a cycle that bound them together. And Abigail's mechanism might continue to revolve around its own love-based temporal axis, on and on, powered by a draught or human breath long after his own train of gears below deck had come to an halt unnoticed.

At last Cox was alone with Abigail's toy, free to assign every sound, every colour and every luminous intensity of his thoughts for her to a particular spring, cog, diamond or ruby. The Emperor of China had commissioned him to build a clock and had then, in all the abundance around him, perhaps forgotten the piece without even glancing at it, thereby returning it to its creator's hands. And Cox had transformed something that was the product of an emperor's whim, and the possibilities afforded by his apparently boundless wealth, into a shimmering memory-laden vehicle which disappeared every evening under a silk cover because He Who Possessed and Reigned Over All did not claim it.

When Cox emerged from behind his folding screen, he struck his companions as unusually content, sometimes even cheerful, a mood in which they had never seen him before. They had also realized that the junk must have sailed out of the Emperor's sight, for whom, as the many bloody tracks his rule had left here and there attested, a clock for condemned prisoners and the end of a human life were more important than its infancy.

Why should a ruler revered as immortal concern himself with the beginning when his power sprang from battlefields, gallows and any place where the end alone was had meaning, and where the blood and lives of subjects, serfs and rebels oozed into the ground?

The Emperor had ordered his English guests to be showered with platinum and white and red gold, silver, brilliants and rubies and any other raw materials they requested and, as strangers to such riches, they had thought that this stream of treasures brought with it a duty to strive with all their might to fulfil a supreme desire. It had surely escaped them that a man who possessed everything could simply forget even the most precious object and not miss it—indeed, that he sometimes even forgot time, which passed even for an immortal lord, never to return.

As the days warmed up and sometimes grew hot and dusty around noon, Cox interrupted his horological work on the second clock movement concealed inside the junk, which he had kept a secret even from his companions, and turned his attention to the contents of the cargo whose lids opened and closed on the finest of steel springs, ejecting fabulous miniature beasts and demons from kegs and chests to mark the hours and the days.

He replaced menacing ghosts and demons with elves and fairies he had cut from polished sheet silver, soldered wings and glorioles of hammered white gold to their delicate shoulders and made constellations of blue sapphires to circle the tip of the main mast as if around the celestial pole, thus extending the mechanics of the child's perception of time to include the motions of the stars. For when Abigail was bored, it was not only time that stood still but also the course of the stars, the sun seemingly riveted to the firmament and the moon frozen in the blackness of night.

Knowing his ember clock was in the safe hands of his companions, Cox could now devote himself in utmost secrecy to Abigail, shielded even from Kiang's eyes by the screen. Every breeze, every breath that billowed the junk's main sail, setting its mechanism in motion and making it chime, was a game that would have enraptured his daughter, now lost beyond all time and space, or would at least have made her laugh.

Cox sometimes thought that he could hear her laughter when the sail swelled with his breath; he heard what had seemingly fallen silent for ever, and for a few instants he felt so dreamily happy that his companions heard him laughing behind his screen, in his painted bamboo grove.

Towards his companions, however, the master became increasingly taciturn. Merlin himself counted more and more days on which Cox addressed not a single word to him other than questions about technical matters and instructions on how to proceed with the ember clock.

How long, the three companions wondered one day on their way home from the workshop through the west gate to their guesthouse and its now blooming garden; how long could a man like Cox survive alone with his memories in his bamboo den? The same Cox who had always been engaged with his surroundings, had always drawn his ideas and inspiration not only from dreams and mourning but also from intercourse with living people and the countless sounds, colours, noises and shapes of the living world.

Might Cox, while his attention was devoted to the silver junk, have suspected that despite all their efforts and months of work, the thing was not flawless enough, not masterful enough for a demigod? Yet some day this piece too would surely be completed, like every previous automaton and clock built, according to the master's designs, at the workbenches here or in Liverpool, Manchester and London—and then, at last, he would return from his silence into their company. Though nothing would ever be the same after what he had endured, he knew better than anyone that time could neither be rewound nor stopped.

Leave him alone, said Bradshaw when Merlin once more re-emerged, frustrated, from the bamboo grove after a vain attempt to engage in conversation with their mute master. We just have to leave him alone. Just leave him.

The early days of summer were rainy, and the Dragon Boat Festival was in full swing; regattas were held to mark the death of a poet who had drowned himself almost two thousand years ago out of banishment-induced despair, and fishermen tossed sticky rice balls and spiced eggs into the water and poured wine on the waves to appease or intoxicate predatory fish and other greedy denizens of the deep in order to prevent them from devouring his corpse.

It was said that Qū Yuán, the unfortunate poet, had rested intact with a stone strung around his neck on the bottom of the Mìluó river in Húnán since the day he had committed suicide during the Warring States period, and his eyes, open for so many centuries, reflected the wave-rippled sky where competing blood-red fleets of dragon boats glided through mountains of clouds on feast days.

Kiang too was worried and was unable to explain why, on the third day of this festival—when music and the strains of merriment were audible even from within the impregnable walls of the Forbidden City—soldiers from the

Imperial Guard began to encircle the English master's house at dawn; mute guards with faces like stone, who over the morning closed ranks to form such a dense cordon that anyone seeking entry to this house, from whichever direction, had to penetrate four rings of heavily armed men standing shoulder to shoulder.

The man whom this ring was intended to protect wished perhaps to check—just as mandarins, flanked by police officers and soldiers, sometimes verified in many of the Forbidden City's palaces and pavilions in the grey light of dawn—whether what was taking place in the darkest nooks and crannies of the long rows of rooms complied with His Radiant Highness's wishes. The only advice Kiang had was that it was best if the only things presently said and done in the English guest's house were what the powers-that-be expected of its occupants.

Woken by the guards' deployment, their voices and crunching steps on the gravel, Cox had stood shivering and watching through the blinds as they formed into ranks, but when his companions arrived for work, the cordon readily and silently parted to allow the surprised clockmakers through. Some of the warriors were standing so close to the workshop windows that their shadows fell on the lathes. Perhaps this was not an inspection but another escort to take Cox back to the Great Wall so that he might identify and rectify on the ember clock case mistakes that Kiang had reported to the authorities or other details subject to secrecy laws.

Whatever might lie ahead, Kiang said, the guests should follow his advice, stay away from the windows and return to work. So now they were sitting obediently at their workbenches—even Cox was with his companions for the first time in a long while. He had removed all tools, filings and glittering components from the silver junk's berth, swept the lathe clean, tossed the silk drape over the pristine-looking ship, left his bamboo grove and, without further explanation, sat down at the common workbench and set about burnishing the ember pans for the fire clock with a mixture of wind-blown sand and finely ground sea salt.

Silently bowed over their activities, neither the English guests nor Kiang spied the five shimmering red-and-gold litters, each carried by eight eunuchs, for which the cordon of guardsmen once more parted before closing behind them again.

For Lockwood, who read from the Bible every evening in a whisper, yet sometimes so loudly and falteringly that Bradshaw or Merlin rebuked him and threatened to stuff his mouth with chamois leather, this sight might have recalled the Red Sea parting before Moses and his Israelites, allowing God's people to stride between towering walls of water over starfish, shells and coral without getting their feet wet . . . But in his fearful anticipation of an inspection by the highest authorities, Lockwood too acted as if he were completely absorbed with the mechanical implementation of an imperial whim, which could make everyone in this workshop rich but also plunge them into one of many chasms of disgrace or, worse, spell their end.

And then this laughter! The clockmakers and their translator, the guardsmen, the dignitaries who had descended from their litters, and even the mockingbirds that had a moment earlier been squabbling on the beaked roofs or asserting new territories with song, suddenly paused, leaving a silence in which nothing but this laughter could be heard—a high-pitched laugh of the kind a child might let out in joy or exaltation.

Then two armed soldiers pushed open the workshop door, followed by a hollow-cheeked man in a green silk robe with an embroidered silver crane across the front. The Englishmen looked up and saw guardsmen kneeling out in the courtyard in the dazzling sunshine, saw the splendid litters, saw banners, spears and a baldachin resembling a dragon's outspread wings in an avenue lined by several rows of alternately kneeling and standing warriors and, last of all, saw a laughing man, accompanied by several women, and heard the Emperor's laughter. Qiánlóng, the Ruler of the World, stepped out of the sunlight into the shadows and across the threshold, and advanced towards them.

Down on your knees! whispered Kiang, already kneeling, his sweat-coated brow pressed to the floor. Yet the English guests did not appear to hear him and seemed paralysed, spellbound by the finery around them.

Qiánlóng was wearing a robe woven from purple silk and golden thread, embroidered with dragon claws and azure bands of cloud, and he laughed at every word spoken to him by one of the women at his side, perhaps as part of a word game or riddle. The barely less finely clad ladies-in-waiting also giggled blithely, as if they were accompanying not the Emperor of China but a lover, a friend or a brother, in any case a jovial man in a buoyant mood, of whom perhaps some anonymous, distant foe must be afraid but no creature in his vicinity.

The guardsmen waited outside in the sun, but they had drawn their ring so tightly around the house that they could have leapt to the Lord of a Thousand Years' defence in a single breath.

Qiánlóng had indeed entered the English master's lodgings without bodyguards, laughing and accompanied by only five of his more than three thousand concubines, whose life's work consisted of preserving their most precious possession—their beauty—and, together with the laughing man's forty-one wives, transforming the Forbidden City into an earthly paradise for a few hours or for nights on end.

How small His Holy Highness was. He should surely have towered over any giant, but he was barely a head taller than his wives, and now he walked towards the kneeling, perspiring Kiang and ordered him, in a voice that once more dissolved into a spate of laughter, to translate for the English master the word that was currently passing from the lips of one concubine to the next in the round. The game apparently involved coming up with as many rhymes as possible for a word, name or term that the Emperor tossed to the laughing group.

Kiang was the only person in the room on his knees. Cox, Merlin, Bradshaw and Lockwood all sat as if pinned to their workbenches by surprise, as if unable to grasp that the law could genuinely require them to kneel and touch their foreheads to the floor before a laughing man in the middle of a word game. Were not mirth and profound reverence so wholly unalike that to conflate the two must prove a fatal error, a mistake every bit as calamitous as to try to quench a fire with oil or a ladleful of mercury?

When the Ruler of the World laughed, did it not behove whole continents to join in with his laughter, whether on their knees or standing upright and at the top of their voices? On the other hand, it might be an unforgivable insult towards His Sublime Majesty even to smile without his permission. No mandarin or master of ceremonies was there to advise them, and Kiang was kneeling, sweat-soaked and mute, before the Emperor and his mistresses.

Now the women also turned to the translator, as if it were his turn to add a new word to their game. Kiang did not dare to return any of the gazes he felt on his skin like falling embers. And then, at last, he uttered the word that the Emperor had ordered him to translate, but he said it so quietly that one of the women tugged gently, almost fondly, on his waist-length plait as if it were a bell-pull and urged him with a giggle to repeat what he had just whispered, louder, louder! And Kiang again whispered the English words, which was merely an alien sound to the Emperor and his mistresses and, though comprehensible, utterly puzzling to the guests: *Monkey King*.

Again, giggled the concubine. Again!

Monkey King, Kiang said once more, staring past Qiánlóng into the distance as if with thes words he had just pronounced his death sentence.

One of the five companions, possibly the youngest yet undoubtedly the most elegant, was dressed from head to toe in silk of the same azure hue as the cloud whorls on the Emperor's red-gold robe; she attempted to repeat Kiang's English translation. In doing so she lent the syllables a wholly original rhythm, giving the word such an exotic ring that three of the Englishmen smiled. Only Cox remained stiff, for the person who had spoken so liltingly and whose cheek the Emperor now gently caressed—as if the vibration, the amplitude, even the temperature of the foreign word might still linger on her features—was the girl who had glided past him on the Grand Canal, the girl in the procession of litters in the bloodied snow, the most remote beauty who had ever crossed his sight—bright, radiant, unattainable.

Did this girl remember, did this woman, in whose features, as if in a misted-up mirror, he thought he could make out both Abigail's and Faye's comeliness, remember . . . Did this princess remember—Cox did not yet know any better and could only regard these women as princesses; did this fairy-like beauty remember their meeting one autumn day in the middle of the Grand Canal? Did she recognize the Emperor's English guest as he sat there, unable to move?

Her eyes brushed him, brushed the companions and seemed, with a highly tuned acuity, to take in everything there was to see in the broad band of sunlight falling through the open door, but they immediately flitted on, as if she had an official, precisely calculated period of attention allotted equally to each and every object and creature; so her gaze flitted over Cox and the frozen group of companions at the workbench, over the golden watchtowers of the fire clock Lockwood had just filled with wood ash to test the accuracy of the scales under the ember pans, and finally snared in the bamboo leaves of the folding screen, to which she now pointed. Her gesture was unambiguous: What is behind there?

Kiang had still not heard a word authorizing him to get up again and so he crawled on all fours towards the screen, as if obeying a command made only to him, until one of the women called out that he should stand up and move like a human being rather than a drowsy whelp. So he got to his feet at last and pushed the screen aside, but stood next to it, bowing deeply, to be close at hand if what he had made visible did not meet expectations. A thing. A thing hidden under a silken drape, waiting to be revealed. Kiang could not see the Emperor's countenance from his low, bowed position, but he sensed that Qiánlóng wanted to see everything that was concealed from him and so he pulled the shroud from the silver ship.

The exclamations, words and expressions of delight that greeted this unveiling sounded no less strange than the singsong translation of *Monkey King*. Even the Emperor's lips parted slightly and for a moment it looked as if he wished to join in with his concubines' chorus of appreciation, but he remained silent, stepped up to the junk and beckoned to Cox to approach. The Englishman almost tripped as he attempted to advance and, in his diffidence, bow at the same time. He knew that the few steps towards the silver ship would bring him closer to the beauty from the Grand Canal than he had ever been to any vision in his life thus far.

The women and girls all now thronged around the marvellous piece, and Cox sensed his work smock, sparkling with silver and white-gold filings, brush the blue folds of his princess's silk robe, and he had the sensation that it was his skin that had been touched, raising goose-bumps under his shirt.

He thought that this sensual thrill must surely be visible on his face and apparent to everyone in the room, even the Emperor. The courtesans did indeed glance at him and laugh, but not because the English master was shivering—no one had noticed his smock brushing against a robe—but because he was blushing for no obvious reason, blushing like a boy caught red-handed.

Sorry?

Cox hadn't been listening.

Although the most rapt attention, even devotion, was required in His Sublime Majesty's presence, Cox had not been listening. Someone had clearly said something to him. A man's voice had addressed him from somewhere.

Was it Merlin's voice? Kiang's? The Emperor's?

One of the courtesans giggled more loudly than the others. But the one whose robe was still touching his smock did not look at him. Her wandering gaze seemed to have alighted on the silver ship.

You are to present this ship to the Lord of Ten Thousand Years, Kiang repeated, no louder yet more urgently than before. You are to show the Lord of Ten Thousand Years how this junk measures and ploughs through time.

Cox spoke, and he heard himself talking as if in a day-dream. The women, his companions, Kiang and His Radiant Highness all shrank; yes, they shrank as he spoke, at a similar speed and to a similarly tiny size as he had when taking shelter in the thicket of his fur saddlecloth during the archer's attack near the Great Wall. Everyone in this room, in the junk's harbour, became miniature fig-ures, passengers on a silver toy ship belonging to Abigail whose commander was none other than himself—the tin-soldier-sized Master Cox.

So he hoisted the sail and reefed it in a little to demon-strate how smooth and easy each manoeuvre was to exe-cute. He dropped the anchor, then raised it, albeit without mentioning its role in winding the second clock concealed below deck; he spun the wheel and moved the rudder blade through all its settings, opened hold hatches and made elves, fairies and guardian spirits pop out of crates, baskets and chests; he inhaled deeply and became the wind that filled the sails and set the course of childhood in motion. Gun ports sprang open to reveal white-gold cannon barrels from whose gaping muzzles—after an interlocking of delicate cogs—trickled rock crystal dust, producing a white shimmer reminiscent of spray on the workbench's wooden sea.

Now the Emperor also clapped his hands, which sported not a single sparkling ring, smiled and had Kiang tell the assembled Englishmen: Zhèngtŏng's flagship! Zhèngtŏng's flagship has risen from the waves.

Not until the evening of that early summer's day, long after Qiánlóng and his ladies, the guardsmen outside the house, and the concerned waiting mandarins, secretaries and eunuchs had once more vanished like ghosts whose appearance nobody, no human, could possibly believe— the Lord of Ten Thousand Years in the Englishmen's workshop! Kiang later explained His Sublime Majesty's exclamation to the English guests.

Centuries ago, when Zhèngtŏng, an emperor of the Ming dynasty, which Qiánlóng's ancestors had always detested, was at the height of his power, he had ordered his huge ocean-ruling fleet to be set ablaze and sent to the bottom of the sea—huge armoured ships, with up to six hundred seamen at arms on each—because he was convinced that China's lustre had grown so dazzling and so far-reaching that this light would attract the rest of the world to undertake a pilgrimage to the throne in the

Forbidden City, pay tribute and offer him their fealty. Of what use could further sea battles, seafaring and voyages of exploration be?

Of course there were, Kiang would later add in response to Cox's fretful enquiries that evening; of course there were other versions: the fleet had been set on fire and sunk because Zhèngtŏng's star was already waning, his empire in decline and the stream of money for this invincible fleet had run dry. But the tale of lustre and splendour, a belief in China's overwhelming might, nay invincibility, had ultimately been the most powerful story of all and therefore still prevailed over every other explanation many centuries after the Mings' demise, transforming the flagship into a symbol of a force that could be destroyed by the Emperor's will alone, not by any earthly foe.

Zhèngtŏng's flagship. Cox had to stop himself from obeying an impulse to stay the Emperor's arm—to touch the Emperor!—when all at once Qiánlóng reached for the junk with both hands, picked it up and puffed into its slack sails, then turned to one of the concubines and pressed the silver ship to her breast like a sparkling babe-in-arms, as the countless gemstones scattered a spray of refracted light; he did this not like one presenting a gift but merely like someone in need of a submissive helper, a maid, a servant. Here, this one will carry the toy. And yet this presentation appeared to cause the other women's white-painted, gold-dusted faces to twist with envy and bitterness. Why her? Why not me?

Only on the face of the girl, the princess of the Grand Canal, did Cox believe he spotted something like a condescending smile, as the woman whom the Emperor had designated to carry the ship was obviously so surprised that she had to take a quick sideways step to keep her balance under the precious object's weight. Fearing that his work might clatter to the ground and be damaged or scuttled, Cox again felt the urge to leap to the courtesan's aid and assist her.

Sensing the threat to his ward should he touch a creature to whose body only the Emperor might lay claim, Kiang gave Cox's smock such a violent tug that metal filings trickled from its folds, breaking all contact with the silk robes of the beauty from the Grand Canal.

And then, cradled in the courtesan's arms, the silver junk did indeed float and sail ahead of His Supreme Majesty and his mistresses like a flagship. Out of the workshop's muted interior, illuminated only by filtering stripes of sunlight, it bobbed into the dazzling noontime and towards the pleasure gardens of the Pavilion of Women under sails swollen by summer breezes and the gazes of mandarins, guardsmen and the silently assembled subjects—the maiden voyage of a ship whose only cargo was time as experienced by a child, propelled into the river of time by a second hidden clock that was connected to the cogs of childish immortality: its creator's mechanical heart.

The brightly coloured pageant of the gleaming craft sailing slowly from its docks and disappearing from the Englishmen's sight for ever may have been unforgettable, but it was that day's unprecedented and even scandalous events that ingrained themselves in the court's memory. Had His Radiant Highness truly forgotten the laws of his dynasty by entering the English guests' house without his bodyguard, without his mandarins, his secretaries and eunuchs, accompanied, but not protected, by only five concubines—five whores!—and exposing himself there, defenceless, to foreign eyes and foreign ears and associating with craftsmen from a barbaric Western land?

Cox's mind, however, retained nothing but rapidly fading scenes and sensations of ethereal volatility that were weightless compared with the pure sound of a name he learnt from Kiang that same evening, when he could no longer hold his tongue but found himself *compelled* to ask.

Ān. The girl's name was Ān. It was Ān that he had seen in the middle of the Grand Canal and in the blood-stained snow outside the workshop windows.

A princess, though? said Kiang. A princess? No princess. A courtesan by rank; no more than a concubine, one of many.

But there was no gossip—this Cox would also find out that very night—no gossip and no rumour in the Forbidden City containing even the faintest doubt that His Sublime Majesty, the Lord of the Horizons, loved this woman more than any other, and one day, shorn of all tokens of her present status, she might be transformed into an empress. No doubt either that anyone who came too close to this love must crumble into dust or be torn asunder by the consequences of his sacrilege.

For to any man other than the Emperor, Ān was a star cruising many light years away, appearing and disappearing from the heavens according to the incomprehensible laws of celestial mechanics.

10

LÌ XIÀ

Into the Summer

There were reports of an uprising by Muslim rebels in the province of Gānsù, watered by the Huáng Hé river. Thousands upon thousands of His Sublime Majesty's subjects had been driven from their villages and towns and were now fleeing. However, while the rebels built pyramids of skulls from the severed heads of hundreds of imperial horsemen, and transformed entire cities into graveyards in the name of Allah, the court set to work in armouries, wardrobes, art collections and storehouses to prepare its relocation from Běijīng to the summer residence in Jehol.

The Invincible One wished to spend another summer in the dust-free, invigorating air of mountains on the fringes of Outer Mongolia and there add to the collection of poems whose calligraphic transcription he began every day long before sunrise. The two chroniclers responsible for keeping the Emperor's personal statistics counted three thousand six hundred and eighty-seven poems at this time.

A horseman from the land of Kham, the eastern region of Tibet, reached the Forbidden City at the same time as news of the rebellion in Gānsù, and, between repeated fits of sobbing, declared that insurgent Khampas had hacked off the hands and feet of a troop of imperial surveyors before ripping their bowels from bellies slit with swords and casting them to woolly pigs to gorge upon before the eyes of the mutilated but still-living men. Yet even this sole survivor's report could neither disrupt nor thwart the court's preparations.

(These and similar messages were, however, only ever passed on in a whisper and exclusively within the army and the secret services, for the mandarins made sure that any prattler who undermined trust in Qiánlóng's invincibility and spread gossip beyond such circles and into the streets had his tongue cut out or molten iron poured down his throat from a beaked ladle.)

No, no rumour or military report crossing the vast expanses of his realm could dim the Emperor's happy anticipation of the clear air of Mongolia and his ancestral Manchurian homeland. His generals were to deal with rebels in some barbarian wilderness until he ordered them to return the command to his hands. The Emperor's progress into summer was as relentless as that of the season itself.

While Qiánlóng made decisions about equipment, art and clock collections, wardrobes, carpets and books—primarily clocks and books—which were to be transported in the endless procession of a relocation train divided into nineteen sections, his closest advisers heard him repeatedly wax lyrical about the deep emerald green of the valleys, gentle mountaintops ringing with birdsong and the crystal waters of the river in which the warmth of hot volcanic springs aroused in anyone who bathed there unspeakably joyous memories of the time when they floated safely in their mother's womb and through which they had perceived the noise of the world as distant, gentle music.

In Jehol, Qiánlóng, who was not only his empire's greatest warlord and poet but also its supreme architect, had dozens of temples and palaces built along the riverbanks for his own summer pleasure, all of them designed to evoke something higher and more magnificent than man. And as he sat in bed over his calligraphy in the early morning hours, he had invented names for all these structures of his own devising and penned poems about these dreams made architecture; indeed, he had turned the structures themselves into verse and transformed wood and stone into poetry:

Pavilion for Listening to Waterfalls

Bridge of the Fir-Scented Wind
Cloud Gate for Greeting the Dawn
Temple of the Flower Spirit
Pavilion for the Pacification of Distant Lands . . .

In Jehol there was no tower, no wall and no gate whose existence, proportions and name had not originated in the Emperor's fertile imagination.

It therefore sometimes appeared to the interpreters of the Emperor's wishes as if Qiánlóng retreated for the summer months not only to his ancestors' homeland but also into the depths of his consciousness whose immeasurable splendour and diversity were materialized in the architecture of Jehol. As if reinvigorated by peaceful slumbers laced with buoyant dreams, he could then return to the Forbidden City in the autumn and fan the heart of the empire with the cooling breezes of his Manchurian home.

More than a hundred species of birds, Kiang enthused about their destination to the English guests as they packed, nested on the banks of artificial lakes so skilfully devised that they might be mistaken for natural bodies of water. Their territorial songs only accentuated the peace and intensity of the morning silence that the Emperor vaunted in his poems; and when the evening wind lifted, producing a melodious murmur in the tops of the fir groves planted around the palaces, then it was as if all the birdsong and even the sound of hammers and the barking of angry or scared dogs combined to form one polyphonic, harmonious cosmic hum and a sense of peace that nothing could disturb.

During the weeks of preparations, the court resembled a beehive or the citadel of a colony of leafcutter ants whose silent workers transported the most incredible, wobbling loads back and forth on their heads.

Courtyards which otherwise lay quiet and empty in the sunshine were now thronged with people shuttling this way and that though never leaving the strictly prescribed routes: porters and litter-bearers, animal-tamers, ostlers, shepherds and valets laden with bags of clothing and crates filled with the finest tea sets, as well as gymnastics teachers and other more mysterious staff carrying leather trunks and cases containing telescopes and microscopes manufactured by Dutch and Italian opticians, and other instruments about whose purpose the baggage train could only speculate.

In total, the train would number four thousand five hundred people on horseback, on foot and in litters or red-lacquered and gilded carriages, a procession barely distinguishable from afar— for instance, from the observatories and watchtowers on the ridges around Běijīng—from a campaigning army, and which, due to its voracity, was hardly less feared in the lands along its route than any enemy bent on plunder.

The clockmakers, the automaton-builders were also to proceed with the court into the summer. After all, work on the clocks had to continue under the Emperor's benevolent gaze rather than in the distant capital where it might be disrupted by unforeseen interference, a shortage of materials or xenophobic scheming by suppliers. For many of the remaining officials shook their heads at the privileges afforded to the English guests. Had European princes and even kings not previously tried in vain to purchase a reception in the Forbidden City? And now craftsmen, incapable of pronouncing correctly a single word of the national language, travelled daily between their quarters and their master's workshop, as if the heart of the empire were a playground that one might enter and leave at will . . .

The vanguard of the procession into the summer set out one muggy morning amid boiling clouds of dust that dispersed only sluggishly in the windless avenues, while the sections that were supposed to bring up the rear were still busy packing the most delicate porcelain, glass figurines and vases painted with the Emperor's dreams into crates lined with down and cotton. Each section would be the vanguard of the next and thus, train by train, prepare the ground so that those that followed would find everything running as smoothly as if there had never been a winter break.

Jehol had lain for months in a kind of slumber during which all operations other than the essential systems had been put on hold—not for reasons of thrift but because Qiánlóng, the greatest architect and builder on the globe, was convinced that, like every organism, buildings, palaces and even temples required time to recover, periods of rest and dreaming when the halls, corridors and gardens were to be free of footsteps and human voices, and even the sewers should run only with pure rain and meltwater.

Two days before the order of departure had finally reached the section with which the English guests were to carry their tools, materials and the almost-completed ember clock to Jehol, Kiang reported to the workshop, and, without further explanation, bade Cox and Merlin to come with him. A covered litter brought them to a courtyard Cox had never entered before and at whose distance from his house he could only guess: the swaying journey had lasted barely ten minutes. The surrounding silence suggested that they had not left the Forbidden City, but the blinds, painted with jasmine blossoms and dragon scales, could not be opened. Nobody except for a few select individuals, said Kiang, as a guardsman opened the litter door outside a spacious, dim pavilion; nobody should be able to memorize the route to the places where the Lord of Ten Thousand Years stored his cherished objects.

His cherished objects? His treasures? asked Merlin.

The Emperor's love could make a gem of even a dry leaf that sailed down from a treetop into a sky-reflecting puddle and become a life-saving raft for a drowning beetle, said Kiang.

Although Cox and Merlin were familiar with the fabulous accounts circulating in London for many years now of Qiánlóng's passion for clocks and all kinds of chronometers, and Cox & Co. had for virtually as many years been one of various purveyors feeding this passion, they were both stunned by what they saw in the half-darkness of the pavilion. Table clocks, pendulum clocks, long-case clocks, water clocks and sandglasses, even sundials made from hammered and embossed gold sheet, which, when lit by a circle of now-extinguished torches, could *effortlessly* imitate a sunny day, whatever the season, and hundreds, many hundreds of mechanical works on pedestals, under glass covers or in cabinets constituted a sort of museum of measured time that included a collection of machines whose workings even such master craftsmen as Cox and Merlin could only surmise.

Deep in this room where cog wheels, springs and pendulums ticked and whirred and whispered by the light of lanterns which made these precious objects look as if they were floating on rafts or islands of light, Cox also spotted that gleaming cone, nearly ten feet high, on whose superimposed plates, of decreasing size and increasing magnificence towards the top, hundreds of miniature figures—jade water buffaloes, columns of porters, workers, rice farmers in silver fields, servants, princesses and soldiers—revolved around an empty, completely empty throne at the apex, a diamond-encrusted throne of jade glittering like dew, above which stars and planets floated on gold filaments as fine as hairs, bent into ellipses: a red-gold sun and a moon crafted from mother-of-pearl and silver and, represented by a multitude of diamonds, opals and sapphires, the con-stellations of the northern hemisphere whose apparent movements, driven by a clockwork that reproduced celes-tial mechanics, second after second, day after day and year after year, depicted the course of time. The celestial clock!

Cox glanced at Merlin, but the other man was just as entranced by the sight of this piece which looked more like a shrine or a sanctuary than an measuring instrument. The celestial clock. To the amazement of his old teachers in Manchester, Cox had helped during his early years as a master craftsman to build this marvel, commissioned by the East India Company and produced at the Brookstone & Pommeroy manufactory as a gift that the English trading company intended to present to the Chinese Emperor as part of its persistent search for new markets.

This altar of time weighed as much as a horse and, due to countless complications, many thousands of working hours and the rare materials involved, had driven Brook-stone & Pommeroy to the brink of bankruptcy, as the East

India Company had been unyielding on compliance with the initial cost estimate and the scheduled delivery date.

Alister Cox had ended up buying the manufactory from its despairing owners David Brookstone and Joshua Pommeroy with high-interest loans granted by two London banks, and then, despite the lenders' misgivings, replaced its long-standing name with Cox & Co., making it the cornerstone of his own fast-growing business in Manchester, Liverpool and London.

Maybe Merlin's name would one day replace the Co. in the manufactory's title . . . One day. For the time being, though, Merlin was but one of over nine hundred English clockmakers, jewellers and fine mechanics who hired out their skills on a daily basis to Master Alister Cox. Now, out of the gloaming in the pavilion loomed a monument from Cox's own past: the celestial clock for the Emperor of China, admired and extolled the length and breadth of England, even by fanatics who had never laid eyes on it.

The rumours told during the many years of work on this mechanical marvel—tales about the immeasurable wealth of a Qīng-dynasty ruler revered as a god, about court ceremonies lasting for days, even weeks in a city the populace were barred from entering, rituals more magnificent than any opera—were so incredible, yes, sometimes so uncanny that Cox, who focused on technical challenges, had occasionally wondered if this Emperor and his court, floating on clouds of infinite resources, really existed—or if the East India Company had invented this god-like figure to justify the extortionate cost of a gift that was meant only as advertising or as a bribe to further its business interests.

Two dozen guards under the supervision of a specially trained watchman well versed in the technical requirements, whispered Kiang, had the sole task of winding the clocks in this pavilion according to a strict schedule and then allowing them to rest once a precise running time, calculated by astronomers, had elapsed. And now the men in steel-blue smocks were executing the recurring annual task of packing the Emperor's clock selection—which varied each year but included more than a hundred pieces for this coming summer—in silk lined with cotton wool and down for their journey to Jehol. For the Emperor did not wish to rely on natural cycles such as flowering and wilting, the alternation of light, dusk and darkness, or the length of shadows, but wished, more than anything else, to see the passing of time by his beloved clocks and to *hear* it by their melodies and their mechanical noises and sounds.

Since the celestial clock had arrived in the Forbidden City from Manchester, not a single summer had passed without it being placed in a specially made litter and hauled by thirty men to Jehol and then back to Běijīng at summer's end.

But how wasteful it would be, said Kiang, to have one of this marvel's builders at their disposal and to eschew his advice as to how to transport this precious clock over a distance of more than one hundred and fifty miles. There had never been any doubt that only a litter, only a porter's careful tread, came into consideration, yet the dismantling of the clock into its component parts and its reassembly in Jehol had in the past filled even Běijīng's most skilful fine mechanics with mortal dread, as each was aware that anyone who touched the tiniest cog of this celestial clock was putting his life on the line.

Seven hundred miniature figures made of twenty-one different types of metal, crystal and wood, polished agate, amber and jade, Cox recalled, had been used to build this piece, along with two hundred animals—horses, birds, camels, elephants—ninety tiny trees carved from every species of wood in China, waterfalls, cascades and mountain streams stitched from river pearls—and then, arching over the throne on gold filaments, this firmament of diamonds and sapphires! In addition, the entire cast of this worldscape and all its scenery had to be manufactured and delivered in two exchangeable versions—the first with elements of a Western court ruled by a European Emperor, the second as parts of a Chinese imperial court; and though a vault with stars and planets revolved over both according to one and the same law of motion, the hours of day and night were of differing lengths.

The owner of this clock could play with empires like a child and place on the throne whomever he wanted whenever he so desired, and even name the stars, making them rise and set again in accordance with his mood. No one in the Western world but Brookstone & Pommeroy could have created such a work, it said in a letter from the East India Company to the British monarch. Cox retained a copy of it among his business papers as a secret reminder that the wit and virtuosity which had set this clock in motion was not his master's in Manchester but primarily his own.

And now this wondrous piece, which had often kept him away from his beloved Faye for days and nights during the years it took to construct, even causing him to miss Abigail's birth one winter's evening, stood before him in the half-light of the pavilion and, as Kiang whispered as solemnly as if they had been in a church or a temple, Merlin and he were to prepare it for travel—ready to be carried out of the Forbidden City to Jehol by thirty of the strongest eunuchs.

On the morning of their departure, after four days of exhausting work on the celestial clock which had eventually been packed into two dozen crates and caskets, it began to pour with rain. Within an hour of leaving the Forbidden City, the litter-bearers were wading ankle-deep through mud along stretches of road trampled and churned by the preceding sections.

Merlin and Cox had often ridden long distances in England and were much happier on horseback at present than in a litter where the monotonous chanting and panting of the porters was the dominant sound, but it was the first time that Lockwood and Bradshaw had taken to the saddle. However, the unexpected honour being shown to them, lowly as they were, soon became torture: by late afternoon, both were saddle-sore. They were helped from their mounts and directed to passably comfortable seats on a covered wagon drawn by six buffaloes, and piled high with carpets rolled up in oilcloth and crates packed with vases. In the tense atmosphere created by the persistent rain and boggy ground, even Kiang did not dare to enquire whether any of the courtiers would agree to accommodate an Englishman in his spacious, sumptuous litter.

By the mandarins' calculations, the journey to Jehol ought to take seven days, seven days at the most, and throughout this time a column of replacement bearers was kept in reserve, since no march into the summer had ever been completed without some eunuchs dying of exhaustion from the weight of the precious loads they had to haul without uttering a groan of complaint or effort.

If the litter-bearers sang in the streaming rain, as the strain made the blood pound in their veins, it was mainly because in these *hauling songs* their forbidden panting and struggle for breath could be disguised as the chorus or the start of a couplet and go unpunished.

When the rain ceased on the fifth day of travel and, on the sixth, mist began to rise in drifting and floating veils between undulating, thickly wooded hills and ridges over a river heated by volcanic forces, and from these veils the distant pagoda roofs and towers of Jehol emerged, the clock caravan stopped.

The singing and with it the panting of the bearers fell silent. The caravan's commander, a corpulent Manchurian who had appeared like a ubiquitous demon at the slightest drop in pace over the previous days and whom Kiang knew stood higher in His Radiant Highness's favour than almost any other court official, ordered the train to halt and his crier to bark out that this sight—this sight!—was the supreme reward compensating every pilgrim and walker for his exertions on the road to Jehol.

Admittedly, the porters and litter-bearers seemed less partial to this supreme reward than to the rice liquor the fat Manchurian ordered to be poured from large wicker-clad demijohns, while his crier shouted that Jehol was proof that the Lord of Ten Thousand Years was capable of enhancing even the work of the gods.

The travellers were to raise their eyes, open their ears! They should all raise their eyes and gaze upon the glittering reservoirs casting back the image of the crystalline skies, crisscrossed only by flower fragrances and capering birds. They should marvel at the fleets of cloud ships, the scraps of mist and the feathery cirrus, messengers of the stars!

Before they once more took up their burdens and solemnly covered the last thousand steps separating them from Jehol and its splendours, they should listen to the roar of the water and the fir forests. Everyone! All of them should raise their heads and listen, unless they wanted to lose their ears and their heads on an executioner's block beside the hot river.

Listen! They should listen to the music of the wind in the branches of the conifers and on the waves, the music of this paradise created by the Lord of Ten Thousand Years where the hubbub, every vain sound of this accursed world died away.

II

ĀISHÌ

Loss

Balder Bradshaw, the ninth of eleven children born to the whitesmith Tyler Bradshaw and his wife Aelfthryd in the county of Lancashire, died within sight of paradise at the age of twenty-nine.

He had spent the whole day in a fresh but painful attempt to take renewed advantage of the privilege of riding and stay upright in the saddle, braving chafe marks that had barely healed during his days of travelling on a water-buffalo cart. Cox and Merlin, who rode sometimes ahead of him, sometimes behind him on his death day, had occasionally tried to correct his posture before the Manchurian gave the signal to halt because the view of distant, mist-shrouded Jehol was apparently more beautiful than anything the caravan had encountered on their march into the summer thus far. Listen! The caravan must stop and listen. The Manchurian raised his cupped hands like shells to his ears and motioned to the train to follow his example.

No one could later say with any certainty why, but Bradshaw's gelding, a muscular Tibetan gelding, suddenly reared, whinnying, onto its hind legs and bolted at a panicked gallop. Some of the litter-bearers claimed to have seen a small furry animal, a fox or maybe a wolf cub, dart between the horse's hooves. Others were convinced that some large horseflies had alighted on a spot rubbed raw by the saddle girth and stung the gelding; it was certainly the season for horseflies and they were driving both the grazing cattle and the carthorses mad.

The only one who presumably knew the truth—a water-bearer who slaked the thirst of the most valuable animals during the journey from leather pails he carried on a shoulder pole and who had been about to water Bradshaw's horse—remained silent. He too could have only speculated whether what he had seen had indeed caused the death of His Sublime Majesty's English protégé, and he was afraid to talk unbidden. A man under the Lord of Ten Thousand Years' protection could not, was not allowed to die.

It had been the wind. A gust of wind had caught the horse's long, black-brown tail from behind, lifted it up and spread it for a second into a dark hairy fan larger than the tired rider. He felt only the draught and did not notice the ghost at his back. Only the water-bearer and the horse, whose nostrils caught a whiff of the water spilling from the leather pails and looked around at the water-bearer, saw this nameless phenomenon suddenly fly up behind Bradshaw, growing ever larger and more menacing. The gelding whinnied with terror, rose onto its hind legs and sought to escape from the danger by launching into a gallop.

In any case, Bradshaw, still captivated by the view of the city surrounded by gauzy river mist and probably delighted by this respite, a welcome break from the struggle to keep his balance, was flung from the saddle, but rather than tumbling to the mossy ground he caught his left boot in the stirrup and was dragged for at least a third of a mile as the horse dashed through the wilderness. During this panicked escape, he must have struck his left temple so unfortunately and so hard against a rock or the trunk of a tree felled by some long-forgotten storm that he was already dead by the time three mounted guardsmen caught up with the gelding and halted it.

Bradshaw was to be the last of the clock caravan's three casualties whom the journey to Jehol had led not to the Emperor's summer residence and its chorus of nightingales and blackbirds but to their deaths. Yet whereas the other two victims—a carter trampled by his team on a stone bridge, and a litter-bearer who expired from exhaustion—had barely halted the procession and were buried during a break not long enough to water the beasts, after a period of confused agitation and several vain attempts by the Manchurian's two personal physicians to resuscitate the Englishman, the caravan drew to a halt. One of the Englishmen, His Sublime Majesty's guest and ward, was dead.

Although Jehol, with its towers, beaked roofs, temples and hilltop pavilions, appeared to float within touching distance above the banks of mist and could certainly have been reached within two hours, the Manchurian ordered camp to be made at the scene of the accident. The laws of the court required that all movement and all work cease for a day, and no one travel, ride, march or sail any further if a guest of the Almighty Ruler, under His wing and in His shadow, met his fate.

Teams of oxen had to be released from their yokes, litters abandoned and lined up next to one another in rows, and saddles removed from horses and beasts of burden. Even ships on the high seas had to obey this rule and cast anchor or, in stormy weather, reef all their sails save for the one canvas necessary to keep the bow pointing into the towering waves. When death claimed the life of an imperial protégé, all life was to pause for one day.

By the time the first campfires were lit in the gathering darkness and, shortly afterwards, messengers arrived from

Jehol to enquire why the caravan was not entering the city, Balder Bradshaw was resting in a grey silk shroud on a bier beside a granite spur that would loom over his grave the next morning. Against the wishes of the Englishmen, who wanted to take their companion to Jehol and bury him there, the Manchurian decreed that the fallen man should be interred at the site of the accident, in the shadow of the rocky crag, to placate the demons. The fallen rider must lend company to the spirits who had contributed to his death until he had told them his story and acquainted them sufficiently with his life so that they might release him peacefully into a world devoid of time or destinations.

Lockwood tried unsuccessfully to hide his tears behind folded hands as he knelt for almost three hours beside Bradshaw's bier, mumbling prayers and invocations that even his companions could not understand. When Cox finally persuaded him to stand up and return to camp—the Manchurian had become mistrustful of the whispered magic formulas which might bring disaster on the caravan—Lockwood said that this accursed venture in China or Mongolia or wherever else they might have ended up was of no further value, none at all, without Balder. This ill-starred trip was pure punishment now. He wanted to go home.

Merlin, who had worked with both Bradshaw and Lockwood, Cox & Co.'s most talented fine mechanics, clockmakers and goldsmiths, in the Liverpool, Manchester and London manufactories, endlessly running through technical details with them and yet repeatedly mixing up the two men's first names, said nothing that evening. He had stood in silence before Bradshaw's blood-stained corpse, had watched in silence as the dead man was washed by eunuchs and wrapped in grey silk, nibbling at his lower lip until it bled, and was now sitting in silence beside the bier.

Only Alister Cox acted as if, despite his grief and confusion, he might be capable of fulfilling his role as master of the English mission. He listened without any visible emotion as Kiang translated the Manchurian's intentions and decisions, laid an arm around Lockwood's shoulders, trying to console him with the suggestion that their collective work on a new timepiece to rival the celestial clock should be entirely dedicated to Balder Bradshaw's memory, should be a memorial to Balder, and yet he was secretly ashamed when, to his relief, he realized that Bradshaw was the only one of his companions whom he could spare without too much inconvenience. Had the accident befallen Merlin or Lockwood, on the other hand . . . Without either of those men's prodigious skills, Cox would have been unable to finish the near-completed ember clock.

Balder was certainly a gifted mechanic and goldsmith, but what he could do, Merlin and Lockwood and Cox himself could do also. Truly irreplaceable, however, were

Merlin's talents as an inventor of incredible clock movements—pendulum systems, water-, wind- and sand-powered mechanisms—and if, alongside himself, anyone could be described as a virtuoso builder of balance wheels, the beating, whirring or silently racing heart of clocks, then it was Aram Lockwood.

By pooling their skills, the three masters of their arts keeping vigil at their colleague's bier were still capable of transforming an Emperor's wishes and dreams into mechanical reality, because each of them, at every stage of construction, could do Bradshaw's work. Without Lockwood or Merlin, even the Emperor of China could have expected at best a work that surpassed none of the many timepieces the caravan was transporting in padded caskets and chests to Jehol.

Although, to Cox's relief, the loss of one of his best craftsmen did not seem irreparable, he could still hardly bear the idea that Bradshaw was now just as dead and as inaccessible as Abigail—and therefore his sweet little daughter's equal. Nobody, nobody was allowed to be where his Abigail was! Wherever death may have snatched her to, Abigail, his angel, who would be with him until the end of his own life, was irreplaceable, incomparable and unique. No human being, past or future, had ever been so beloved and so sorely missed—or as dead as she was now.

Bradshaw's burial the next morning was almost incidental and would have struck a disinterested observer as part of the general preparations for departure: tents were struck, pack animals reloaded, litters swept of the previous day's dust with marten-hair brushes, water buffalos yoked, the final embers from the campfires smothered with earth and sand to avoid a wildfire—and a foreigner in a silk shroud laid in the shadow of a rock needle in a grave that had been dug deeper than usual when travelling in order to protect the body from the insatiable hunger of Mongolian wolves.

Cox doubted that the Manchurian had really considered this when fixing the burial spot—but it became clear in the light of the swiftly rising morning sun that the shadow of the rock beside which Bradshaw lay interred would henceforth slide across this grave like the finger of a sundial, disappearing, then reappearing morning after morning, and Balder would rest within the compass of a clock governed by celestial mechanics alone.

While three porters filled the trench with earth, sand and the ashes of some arm-thick incense sticks and, on Merlin's instructions, laid flat stones polished by the hot river on top of the mound, carters lashed down the loads, climbed onto coachboxes covered with buffalo leather and manoeuvred their wagons into formation. Only the three Englishmen and Kiang stood idly and silently by, watching the gravediggers work as if their companion's resurrection or their own lives depended on every gesture executed at the grave. Once the last stone had been positioned on Balder Bradshaw's resting place, the Manchurian gave the signal to depart.

The litter-bearers struck up a hauling song, whose more than one hundred verses they were unlikely to need to sing that day: the stage before them was the shortest of their march to Jehol. The golden roofs of the city's pagodas gleamed in the sun, close and enticing, and ought to be reached by noon. Only the odd sliver of mist still hung low over the river's shady banks. Carpets of fallen leaves from the previous autumn bobbed in the sluggish eddies along the banks. Everything suggested a hot summer's day without a cloud in the sky.

Did the nearby city's splendour perhaps stem from the fact that His Sublime Majesty was already in residence, with banners and pennants rippling in the breeze to signal his presence and warn the city's inhabitants to sweep the streets and alleys, scrub their doors and gates with ash lye and remove all refuse and flotsam from the canals and waterlily ponds? Some of the golden roofs glinted as if the craftsmen had only just added the final shingles and dismantled their scaffolding and were now standing in the lanes, gazing up in rapture at their immaculate handiwork. From the distance came the unmistakable sound of a gong being beaten to mark the changing of the guard. Was the Emperor really already in his summer palace?

No one in the caravan or among the army of servants, eunuchs and officials who welcomed the train to Jehol that day was able or willing to provide any information. The Emperor always decided alone when a mandarin was to dispatch a crier onto the platform of the graphite-coated Pavilion of Windless Days, ordering him to announce several times, chanting the message repeatedly like a priest, that the Sun of the Empire's arrival marked the beginning of summer.

His Sublime Majesty alone determined when he wished to be visible and when he wished to be invisible, when he would make a city sparkle through his presence and when this sparkle was mere reflected splendour, signalling little more than that any place in this world must be ready to welcome the Almighty Ruler at any moment if it did not wish to be crushed into dust.

The Emperor's will was accomplished without His Sublime Majesty needing to set foot anywhere: the arriving train dispersed within minutes, disappearing into the palaces of Jehol or outbuildings decorated as palaces, into stables, between ponds and bridges, across squares guarded by stone dragons and through open pavilions. After that, the city, enveloped in shimmering heat, sank back into a silence in which barely a human voice was to be heard. Clearly still unsettled by the arrival of the procession, two dogs yapped in two separate, distant places. Birds sang. They sang whichever way a newcomer turned. The number of singers must have been enormous.

Qiánlóng had had thirty palaces erected beside the hot river and lived up to his title as the Greatest Architect and Builder under the Stars by constantly consolidating, renovating and fortifying these and other residences, in addition to embellishing them with gardens, playgrounds and parks of fairytale beauty. No European had set eyes on the paradise that was Jehol. Without knowing it, Cox and his companions might have been the first; none of them had the faintest diplomatic knowledge, and even the residence's custodians were unable to say if His Sublime Majesty had ever received secret Western emissaries or guests here.

The Englishmen and their translator were assigned to a spacious pavilion that was to be both their living quarters and their workplace by a palace official whom even Kiang had trouble understanding. Kiang translated haltingly that the building had only been completed the previous spring and had thus far accommodated only good spirits, no humans.

The bedchambers and living rooms were painted blue, the two tearooms dark red, the workshops and a steam bath powered by volcanic energy, white: the colours of the air, the clouds, fire and water were to bless and expedite the work to be completed here.

Reached by four decorative wooden footbridges, the pavilion stood like an island in the middle of a lotus pool, in which two black swans were engaged in combat as they arrived.

12

JEHOL

By the Hot River

In the birdsong-filled woods of Jehol, said Kiang as he helped the English guests to stow away their luggage and tools, there lived and bred more than one hundred species of birds from among those pictured in the summer residence's watercolour collections, including songbirds capable of covering, or at least enhancing, virtually any human noise with their love songs and territorial calls. Heated by volcanic springs according to the Emperor's wishes, dreams and whims, the river fed deep-green artificial lakes which had been set in this singing countryside and were designed to reflect skies redolent with fragrances, pollen and swirling flights of birds, like a universe that the Emperor's will alone had commanded to descend from the heavens.

But the clear air of Jehol, said Kiang, pinching some silver screws that had slid from a wooden box to the floor between his thumb and forefinger as if he were imitating a bird . . . It was not only dust and noise that the clear air of Jehol filtered and washed from the summer months but, most importantly, the strain of ruling and the poisons of power, intrigues and expedited tribunals which drowned every breach of the law in raging oceans of blood. There were no judges or executioners in Jehol, for no one who had ever been the subject of a complaint or a lawsuit in the Forbidden City was authorized to enter this residence whose serene summery peace, renewed each year with solemn ceremonies, was disturbed only by the occasional hunt.

So only the most docile subjects were allowed to spend their summers in Jehol? asked Merlin. He was sitting at the window beside which he intended to place his workbench so that he might enjoy the view across floating lotus flowers to pine-covered mountains whenever he glanced up from his work. Only the most docile, the most amenable? Might that not also mean that the population of this city was made up of lickspittles, brainless servants and, above all, ingenious plotters who knew how to conceal their true intentions better than any of their rival courtiers?

A guest should mind his words and thoughts in Jehol too, replied Kiang, suddenly lowering his voice, for here, as in the Forbidden City, the walls had eyes and ears. Here, even a suspect's facial expressions were studied, interpreted and recorded in a report.

Only a question, said Merlin. It was only a question.

But Kiang had already turned back to a shelf where he was supposed to arrange dozens of tins containing many different sizes of silver- and gold-plated screws, right down to the very tiniest, as well as springs and steel pins, and he said no more.

The English guests spent the first seven days in paradise assembling and re-calibrating the celestial clock. The piece's previous custodians, a badly burnt and disfigured master from Běijīng and his grovelling assistants, watched the Englishmen's fluid, swift movements, sometimes with scepticism, sometimes with surprise and admiration. Thus and only thus, Kiang told them, were they to maintain this timepiece in the future.

On the eighth day, when the clock had been fully assembled, as if their work had merely been part of an opening ceremony planned in the Forbidden City, His Sublime Majesty's arrival was announced on the Square of the Cicada Choirs, hailing the start of summer.

Whenever the Emperor entered the Forbidden City or any of his other fortified residences, all eyes were trained on him—or at least on the magnificent litter he was believed to be inside, or on a dragon junk on board which he was said to be travelling. Baldachins floated like flying carpets over the heads of long processions, banners and pennants snapped in the wind, and whole forests of standards and spears rippled over bridges, across parade grounds and along cheering avenues.

In Jehol, however, many laws governing the ruler's comings and goings appeared to be suspended. Here, Qiánlóng came and went as inconspicuously and inexorably as twilight, dawn or nightfall; and his presence only became an undeniable, established fact when it was proclaimed on squares like the Square of the Cicada Choirs.

Moreover, this arrival was associated each time with a new and spectacular sign. One of these signs in the past had been the inauguration of an artificial lake dotted with ornamental islands of purple lotuses, its banks screened during the many months of work involving an army of lake-diggers, gardeners and hydraulic engineers by a temporary curtain painted with the likeness of the original wild surroundings.

Beneath the spidery light of firework bouquets, this curtain had been consumed by flames that seemed to lick the stars. The glowing flakes that tumbled to earth were intended to reveal and illuminate His Sublime Majesty's transformation of a patch of scrubland into a waterscape that reflected the stars, the rosy dawn and unprecedented lakeside gardens.

Another year, at a cue from the Emperor on his invisible throne in Jehol, a waterfall in the dynasty's red-and-gold colours, fed by a hidden mountain reservoir, had gushed from a rock face overhanging the city by the light of a row of flickering, flaming torches. Gushed! from a bare rock face which no gurgling rivulet or stream had ever graced before.

And this time, said Kiang, when he returned one scorching afternoon from an audience with the mandarin whom he was obliged to consult on all matters pertaining to the Englishmen, this time it was the English guests' re-assembly and erection of the celestial clock, the Emperor's favourite toy, that had been designated as the sign of His arrival—the sign of His arrival.

Never before, not even on the day it was presented eleven years ago, had this clock, this gift from the East India Company (which had opened no less than two new trade routes for the English merchants), been in such pristine condition or run with the utter precision with which it had recently begun to work after the attentions of the English master craftsmen.

The Emperor's desire to mark his arrival in summer with the first chime of this clock's bells and to usher in a new season with this sound, said Kiang, was perhaps a sign of the particular favour he bestowed on his guests. For unlike the sensation of a waterfall or the unveiling of a lake amid fiery drama and a shower of ashes, it was the attractions and treasures guarded in strong rooms and vaults, accessible to a very small number of initiates, which had captured the court's—and the people's!—undivided attention and was whipping them into a frenzied state of mind. Even a grey, run-of-the-mill object kept locked away and rarely displayed could acquire an exorbitant, even magical value in this way and exalt anyone who came into contact with it.

An astronomer from Tiānjīn, whose greatest honour in life was his responsibility for the celestial clock's upkeep and supervision, had suggested at one of the many meetings held to prepare the summer that the clock should really be exhibited for one day on the Square of the Cicada Choirs. This marvel should be presented to the people of Jehol as proof that the Lord of Ten Thousand Years not only presided over the beginning and the end of time but also over its calculation and the speed of its passing. No answer had ever emerged from the Emperor's shadowy realm, however, and the astronomer's fear of disgrace had often cost him sleep.

Illuminated day and night by mother-of-pearl lanterns as white as the moon, the celestial clock dominated a windowless part of the Pavilion of Liquid Time reserved for the Emperor alone. No stray ray of sunlight was to damage the splendid colours of the carved or cast-metal characters rotating around an empty throne, nor bleach the glittering outfits of the tiny courtier dolls, the red armour of the miniature warriors, the glorioles of good and evil spirits, the finery of princesses and concubines, the water buffaloes, the rice farmers and the fishermen.

The little throne at the apex of this piece remained empty, always, until the Emperor entered the pavilion and placed at the tip of the world his own likeness, no bigger than a finger, or the even smaller likeness of whichever distant sovereign enjoyed his respect. Over a dozen of these doll rulers lay ready in a casket only the Emperor was authorized to open so that he might set a master of the world of his choice on the throne as an experiment or for his own amusement, and the universe might then, in mockery and for a few revolutions of the mechanism, rotate around this successor.

The tiny number of people who had ever seen Qiánlóng standing, lost in thought, before his favourite toy—some of his wives and concubines, bodyguards, clock custodians and valets waiting invisibly in the dark pavilion for a word or sign from His Sublime Majesty—were reminded of a child at play, occasionally setting the replica of an enemy general or of the commander of rebellious nomads on the clock's rotating tip so as to prove, by means of this timekeeper, how ridiculous, how grotesque and fantastical, any other human being looked on this throne, around which not only *Zhōng Guó*, the Middle Empire, but also Heaven and Earth revolved.

Sometimes it seemed to those who witnessed these hours filled with the varying mechanical whirr and buzz of the cogs as if the Invincible One saw all his adversaries or enemies as mere figurines on the turntables of his celestial clock, relinquishing to them for a few seconds his position at the centre of the cosmos before destroying them.

In the days following their arrival in Jehol, the English guests requested permission to pay a pilgrimage-like outing, one afternoon per week, to Balder's grave. They would then ride to *Balder's Sundial*, as Cox had christened his tomb on their first visit, secretly associating this name with the idea that Balder Bradshaw was still present at the centre of this clock.

Cox went along out of respect for his companions, albeit reluctantly, because these outings stirred up memories of Abigail's grave in Highgate. Only when Balder's tomb gradually faded to a mere monument whose resemblance to a sundial supplanted its original purpose was Cox also ready to forget that one of his finest clock-makers awaited resurrection under the needle of rock pointing into the sky like a clock hand. Resurrection: this was a recurring word in Lockwood's mumbled, sometimes teary prayers beside the grave.

One stormy day in July, when the English guests had finished their preparations and adjustments in the work-shop and, after the time-consuming assembly of the celestial clock, were looking forward to putting the final touches to their ember clock, they were informed by Kiang that His Sublime Majesty was once more entertaining different plans. The English guests were to cease all work for the time being and wait for a signal from the Emperor.

They waited and waited and waited for the Emperor's signal, and August came. And Cox and his companions began to grow accustomed to the idea that the Emperor presumably preferred to spend his leisure with his old, trusty toys instead of with the results of the latest mechanical experiments.

But with the onset of days of steady rain and a mild breeze bearing scents of pine resin, lavender and lotus, came that momentous morning when not only Cox but Merlin too were woken at an hour when the last stars still hung in the western firmament, while in the east the hilltops and soaring mountain peaks around Jehol were silhouetted black against the red and violet of imminent daybreak. It was the end of night.

The Lord of Ten Thousand Years, Kiang whispered into the sleeping men's ears, wished to present a plan, a request, to the masters from England, now, this very moment—not a command, not an order; a request. The Emperor did not order. He requested. It was summer after all, and no area of life in summer should resemble life in the Forbidden City and the other cooler, darker seasons of the year. There were no orders in Jehol.

Cox dressed quickly and anxiously. He knew that the Emperor wrote poetry or read or perfected his calligraphy skills around this time of day, but he knew nothing of Qiánlóng's other early-morning routines which were cloaked in the utmost secrecy. As he and Merlin followed Kiang along corridors and halls, squares and walled gardens, flanked by an escort of guardsmen and eunuchs carrying huge umbrellas, he felt dread at the prospect of a fateful decision or that he might find the Almighty Ruler ill-disposed.

His confusion increased when, in spite of the pouring rain, their route led them down to the riverside and a sandbank. There, a white sail had been pitched, similar to the plain awnings used by lake-diggers and well-builders on hot days. Rivulets of rainwater fell from the edges of the sail like chains of pearls. The mist rising from the river enveloped this shelter, making the unremarkable, almost frail figure sitting there on a cushion, wrapped in a grey shawl and gazing up at the group stumbling down the embankment, appear strangely disconnected, but there was no doubt—it was the Emperor.

He was alone. There may have been immaculately camouflaged guardsmen and bodyguards crouching in the undergrowth for his protection, but to all appearances the Lord of Ten Thousand Years was sitting beside the hot river on his own.

He smiled. He smiled, even though looking into his eyes for even a fraction of a second during an audience was punishable by death. He smiled, and bade the arriving men to raise their foreheads from the wet lakeside sand and get up off their knees. They were to drape the silk shawls close by around their shoulders and take their seats on cushions arranged in a triangle before him: Kiang in the middle, Merlin to his right, Cox on the left—no one but the Englishmen and their translator! All the others were to withdraw beyond the edge of the curtain of water cascading from the sail's edge and make themselves invisible. Qiánlóng wished to be alone with the masters from England and talk to them about clocks and the whisper of time.

The fact that the Emperor was sitting with them, like a shepherd or a fisherman, around a brazier in which pinewood charcoal and two incense cones were smouldering and releasing a delightfully unfamiliar fragrance . . . the fact that the most powerful man in the world was wrapped in a watery lead-grey shawl like those of his visitors and without any insignia of his rank, wishing to distinguish himself from them neither by his posture nor his clothing, a slender, fine-limbed man, but smaller than any of the others in this company, this bothered, indeed unsettled Cox more than the pomp of the court and all the rituals he had seen in the Forbidden City; the Emperor of China not as a godlike, peerless sovereign, but as one of many. A man on the lakeshore, smiling beneath a tarpaulin, waiting patiently until the three visitors had sat down opposite him, as uneasily, as slowly and carefully as if they were aching with pain, as awkwardly indeed as if they were wounded.

If, amid scraps of mist and curtains of rain, His Sublime Majesty were capable of metamorphosing into a man, a mortal barely distinguishable from his subjects, then what metamorphosis might lie in store for clockmakers from London or their speechless translator?

Or . . . Or were all those present actually supposed, for the duration of an audience beside this river on this morning of whispering rain, to be similar, equal even— equal in terms of the space-defying laws of liquid time, which abolished not only all differences between men but also between the organic and inorganic natural world, between every thing and every creature that had ever taken shape or would ever take shape?

For what would ultimately remain of a star, a sun surrounded by a host of planets, asteroids, moons and meteorites whose light had died out billions of years ago? And what of all the other heavenly lights that would arise in the coming eons before bursting apart again over the relentless course of time into a swarm of nameless particles and atomic components which, inconceivably far into the future, under the pressure of forces beyond human imagining, could aggregate into new elementary formations, rotating and growing, and gradually swelling into forms of unheard-of size, unheard-of beauty or ugliness . . . And all of this only to crumble, after their lifetimes had reached their term, into unfathomable darkness?

Only one of the four men gathered around the brazier was at liberty to smile. The others sat without speaking, breathless with awe beside a whispering, rolling river on whose bank the Emperor would, on other, sunny mornings, dip his calligraphy brush into the water and pen poems on the smooth stones. The words evaporated in the warmth of the rising sun, wiping the stones clear again. The Emperor wrote and watched his writings vanish. And he went on writing.

It is raining, Qiánlóng said so quietly that it seemed he was trying not to disturb the music of the water trickling from the tarpaulin and the murmur of the river. It is raining.

His Sublime Majesty had summoned his English guests to the riverbank that morning in order to set out for them a plan compared to which all their previous work—both in the manufactories of their homeland and in the Forbidden City—would seem mere preliminary drills, apprentice pieces or tests of skill. For however artful the little silver ship, the ember clock and other automata and clockworks devoted to the shifting speeds of time that they had designed and built, what Qiánlóng now presented as his wish—no, as his new irrefutable dream—was so grand and yet so familiar, that it was as if he and Cox and his companions had dreamt it together—yes, together; as if they had imagined the impossible so that they might one day surpass the boundaries of reason and logic and make it come true: a clock mechanism capable of measuring seconds, instants, hundreds and thousands of years, and beyond those millennia, the eons of infinite time whose cogs would still be turning when its creators and all their offspring and all *their* offspring had long since vanished from the face of the earth.

A clock that struck out beyond the whole of human time into starry space, never standing still, its sole limits the permanence and mystery of matter itself. For even if the most durable and precious metals and jewels necessary to build such a work of art would also break up into dust and the tiniest, fleeting elements of life at some ineffably distant point in time, it would be only a *thing* that perished, not a physical principle that pointed to a place beyond this finite world.

If there were one sound above all others, said Qiánlóng after he had been silent for so long that Cox and Merlin had shot a questioning glance at Kiang in search of a gesture, a sign that they should get to their feet and leave . . . If there were one sound that best represented the passing of time, then it must surely be the constant whisper of the rain connecting the heavens to the earth. Every strand of rain was a thread stitching the clouds and the firmament to the gardens and rivers, cities and seas and the innards of the earth, from which all of creation forced its way towards the light.

Cox had never felt as close to any sovereign's excesses and claims to omnipotence as he did during those minutes on the riverbank. Along with generations of clockmakers and automaton-builders, he had dreamt, like the Emperor, of trains of gears that ran for ever, on and on, without having to be rewound after the initial impetus: *perpetuum mobile*.

The task that he and Merlin were now being asked to carry out, after the virtuoso samples they had produced in the Forbidden City, had occupied the two of them for many years in London without their really nearing a solution. Yet Qiánlóng's envoys and scouts in Europe had obviously encountered the same rumour that had done the rounds of the Continent's courts, which were obsessed with toys and extravagant status symbols, as well as the circles of fine mechanics who fine-tuned curiosities, automata and other machines: if anyone could be trusted to succeed in the impossible task of developing a *perpetuum mobile*, then it was the London-based master craftsmen Jacob Merlin and Alister Cox. They may not have been lords of time, but they were peerless at measuring it. Qiánlóng's scouts had presumably returned from Europe with these and other similar appraisals. There was probably not an astronomer alive who did not measure the orbits of the celestial bodies and the dynamics of the universe by clocks from one of Cox & Co.'s manufactories. And there was no sea captain afloat who did not rely on the precision of a ship's clock from London, Liverpool or Manchester when charting his course. After a couple of enquiries, therefore, anyone planning the impossible, even a stranger to Europe and the world of mechanics, would have necessarily encountered the names Merlin and Cox.

Before Cox could screw up his courage amid the whispering rain and ask the Lord of Ten Thousand Years if it had truly been the idea of a clockwork that would run for all eternity that had convinced him to summon Cox and his companions halfway around the globe, Qiánlóng said, The movement of this clock . . . It is the movement of this clock that I hear whenever and wherever silence falls. It is the movement of this clock that brought you to this riverbank.

13

SHUIYÍN

Mercury

A clock for all eternity. The clock of clocks. A *perpetuum mobile*.

Had any lord, any ruler or god-like Emperor ever tried to enter the mind and heart of one of his subjects? Or was it genuinely possible that a clockmaker and automaton-builder from England and the Emperor of China, separated not by half a world but an entire universe, might have simultaneously arrived at the same idea? So might some form of spiritual kinship bind this Emperor and this English clockmaker together across oceans, language boundaries and systems of thought? Bind them together! Even though all thought, all laws and all order in this world would appear to drive an unbridgeable chasm between them?

Whatever logic might suggest: since that morning by the hot river, Cox felt akin to the Lord of Ten Thousand Years. Yes, akin. Whatever costumes he wore, whichever titles he bore, this curiously frail-looking yet infinitely powerful man clearly dreamt of similar things, dreamt of a clock whose gearing would continue to turn in a boundless, unfathomable future.

Compared with the construction of such a timepiece, even astronomical celestial clocks seemed like mechanical trifles, all of them eventually coming to a halt and requiring a constant injection of energy, a winder with his key or a servant to pull a chain that sent a pendulum that gravity had drawn to the floor rattling back to the top.

Such timepieces had lost their purpose almost as soon as they had struck their first hour. Time passed these children's toys by unaffected; their parts and cogs stood amid the gently gathering dust for a while, frozen in an everlasting present, before subsiding into rubble and splinters, crumbling over the course of further millennia into ever-smaller elements until they were reduced to the size of the microscopic primeval building blocks of all matter.

But this clock! This clock, though: even if its components were no more able to stand the test of time, the principle of its construction spanned all eternity, for where the cogs of this mechanism were designed to turn, form and shape no longer meant anything and all that existed were the immortal laws of physics.

Wind, water, the sun's warmth, air pressure, thermometric and hygrometric movements . . . Cox and Merlin had spent years in Manchester and London searching for new energy sources that might make a clock to tick for the rest of eternity, for it was obvious from the outset that no spring, no hand-wound pendulum nor the weight of the world could achieve this task.

They had even experimented with a tidal clock near Southend-on-Sea, which was to be kept running by the alternation of high and low tide, driven by the pendulum of the moon. Yet coastlines too were often little more than shifting boundaries, sanding up or drowning as a result of tectonic disasters, the overwhelming power of volcanic activity or simply the never-ending, naggingly effective forces of erosion.

Inspired by the steaming piles of refuse on the banks of the Thames and the vapours spreading a pestilential stench as they rose from the ventilation shafts of the great abattoirs—proof that every form of decay released energy, inexhaustible energy, because everything that existed began to decay from the first second of its life—Merlin had built a gas engine capable of converting this foul odour into power to drive a clock for longer than any previous source of energy had done.

However, like so many of their experiments, this one too was interrupted and scuppered by an order that reached the office in Shoe Lane in a sealed handmade envelope—an irresistible offer they could not turn down. After all, the wages of the goldsmiths and fine mechanics, the many coloured metals, the machines and the rent had to be paid for, and any promising experiment could lead only to hollow success, a success that would take many years to generate a profit.

This time, a silver swan capable of stretching its neck, beating its wings and even uttering a form of song needed delivering to Saint Petersburg. A silver swan with coal-black eyes of polished onyx. The Tsar was ready to pay a fortune for it, a fortune for a risible, worthless plaything. But still they built it.

Having removed all the other clocks from his house, Cox had carried out secretive trials at Abigail's tomb in Highbury cemetery with a mechanism driven by the heat and gases produced by organic decomposition. A clock no larger than an aster blossom, set into Abigail's gravestone amid a cluster of Bourbon roses, was to be powered by thermal energy and by the silently advancing process of decay below ground, displaying what was left of his daughter's life on a clock dial.

Cox wanted to be able to read the swift passing of his remaining days from the transformation of Abigail's sweet nature into the original elements of life—transformation!, not decay, not decomposition. Even though his workshops continued to manufacture the finest automata as well as table and pendulum clocks, Abigail's *life clock* became the only chronometer that conferred a semblance of meaning on Cox's life. To anyone puzzled by this grave ornament, he would say that it befitted a horologist's daughter and made a more dignified decoration for her final resting place than a stone angel or cast-iron laurel leaves.

Yet nobody, not even Faye or Merlin, had ever known about the bundles of extremely fine glass and copper tubes reaching down into the darkness, connecting this clock to the clayey soil and transmitting kinetic energy to a delicate balance wheel.

Merlin had surely guessed, but he had never asked. And Cox had always felt a small measure of consolation as he stood beside the grave and watched the hour hand creep around the clock inserted in the stone. It was Abigail, after all; it was molecules—tiny, immortal particles of her body—that were driving this timepiece and keeping the memory of her voice, the warmth of her hands and the lustre of her eyes and hair alive. Even if the hands of this clock would not rotate for ever and ever around a shaft driven by the particles of life, hope remained that it would outlive its constructor and continue day after day to mark the hour of Abigail's death with a delicate chime once England's greatest mechanic and automaton-builder had followed his daughter's path out of time.

Merlin felt just as liberated as Cox by their new assignment from the Lord of Ten Thousand Years. After all, both had continually pursued the *perpetuum mobile*, the ultimate utopian goal of the horologer's art, either in total secrecy as Cox had done in Highgate, or in defiance of every rule of business and at their own, incalculable expense. Even the prizes offered by the odd madcap aristocrat and the Royal Academy, several decades ago, for the invention of an ever-chiming clock would have paid, at most, for the necessary fundamental research. But now . . .

Now the Emperor of China had given them an assignment and unlimited funds to accomplish it. Anyone who had laid eyes on the elegant grandeur of a single palace in the Forbidden City or the construction plans for the summer residence at Jehol, which had sprouted in the wilds of Mongolia, or the crenelated course of that Great Wall, snaking over mountain chains and across steppes and deserts and protecting China for centuries from the barbarians, knew that the master of all these wonders of the world was both able and willing to pay stratospheric prices to realize his dreams; pay them in gold, time, labour—and human lives. In the shadow of each wonder of the world lay a mass grave. Whatever there was to be had in this world, at whatever price, the Emperor of China would have it.

Cox and Merlin began to draw up lists, long calculations and details of materials, precious objects and simple things they needed to build an eternal clock: mahogany and polished glass, steel, lead, brass, bars of platinum, gold and silver, glass flasks, gilded pendulum chains, diamonds, rubies—and mercury. First and foremost, mercury. One hundred and ninety pounds of mercury.

During the long journey on the *Sirius*, Cox had offered to provide the most precise air-pressure measurements ever taken during such a voyage to a group of natural scientists from Oxford who were sailing to Japan to research Asian monsoon currents. For Cox & Co.'s barometers not only graced instrument tables in weather stations around England, they were also among the manufactory's most popular export items. This was because, ultimately, a barometer was a means of seeing into the future—it allowed one to draw conclusions about the clouds, wind strength and the risk of imminent storms from the rising and falling of a column of mercury.

And as the columns of numbers, measured and noted five times per day, grew ever longer, Cox and Merlin had revived an idea they had come up with during their quest back in England for suitable natural forces to power a clock; an idea they had not rejected but merely shelved due to its complexity, its cost and the mechanical obstacles.

Air pressure! Using the rising and falling air pressure that set a mercury meniscus in motion as a clock pendulum. There would be variations in pressure, caused by climatic or local weather conditions, for as long as an atmospheric shield protected the Earth from meteorites and other projectiles originating in space, for as long as clouds sailed across the blue expanses of this shield, for as long as the fertility-bringing monsoon watered entire continents and the trade winds swelled the sails of merchant vessels and warships alike. Should the globe lose its shield, that was the end of the world and of terrestrial time. There would be no more years, no more seconds to measure, but until then . . .

Until then, a clock that drew its energy from variations in air pressure could divide human history into large and tiny phases, and indicate when one life or era began and another ended.

Cox cherished the memory of that afternoon on the *Sirius* when the sail of a barquentine that had come flying over the horizon turned out to be a British warship rather than a privateer, a pirate or the flagship of a hostile fleet. He had been sitting in the sun on the quarterdeck with Merlin, making a rough estimate of how much mercury a flask would need to contain for it to move a set of weights and thus a drive wheel.

Their calculations showed that a change in weather that caused air pressure to rise or fall by only one unit could power a mechanism for over sixty hours. And when one considered that in one day such a change in pressure occurred many times—countless times! Cox recalled that he had proffered a few numbers and drawn the resulting conclusions that afternoon—the first mate had just shouted that the distant sailing ship was tacking a course under British colours, not the Jolly Roger—and that

Merlin stood up, walked over to him and, for the one and only time in their lives, embraced him.

The helmsman in whose field of vision the two crazed passengers stood attributed their joyful embrace to the relief the two of them obviously felt at the first mate's all-clear and altered their course two strokes to port on the captain's orders, as an artist accompanying the natural scientists from Oxford wished to get a better view of a school of dolphins prancing in the *Sirius*'s bow wave.

One hundred and ninety pounds of mercury . . . It was not new to their suppliers that the English clockmakers were entitled to ransack whole hoards of treasure for their automata, but mercury! Even Kiang had to scour his dictionaries to translate this demand and was surprised to find that the raw material shared its name with a planet—the winter light. For the court astronomers, this orb was nothing but a lightless star, as black as the sea on a moonless night, and its realm was icy, wintery darkness.

Kiang did not dare to voice his first idea of a possible source of this element. It would have meant suggesting the stripping of a shrine; during the construction of the summer residence, along with the other imperial palaces in Jehol, a pavilion had been built whose roof formed an ebony vault like a starry sky above a sort of miniature landscape, a model of Zhōng Guó, the Chinese Empire, in granite, basalt, marble, rock crystal and quartz sand. This model, whose surface area Cox compared in his mind to the dimensions of the nave of St Paul's Cathedral in London, showed the relief of all the empire's mountain ranges, fertile plains, deserts and steppes, its seas, lakes and rivers, all its cities and fortresses . . . And its borders, true to scale, were continually shifting, expanding or being refortified in line with military conquests, disasters or political alliances.

Hence the borders ran in this direction or that, recoiling from embattled regions and giving the model the appearance of an organism, a jellyfish or an amoeba, lying there like a breathing, shape-shifting creature in the narrow strips of daylight or moonlight falling through the pavilion's gilded arrow-slits in a lattice of light, like lines of longitude and latitude on a globe.

And across practically this entire miniature world ran the Great Wall, Wàn lǐ cháng chéng, the Ten-Thousand-Times-Unimaginably-Long Wall, twisting and turning this way and that countless times according to the military situation, as if this, the largest structure in the history of humankind, were, along with its many other functions, meant to instil meaning into the wall's popular name, *Great Dragon*, whose extraordinary dimensions both protected and dominated the Middle Empire.

This dragon had devoured armies of stonecutters, masons, porters, carpenters, brick-makers and other craftsmen who had died from exhaustion, disease, hunger and beatings over the centuries it took to build. Millions of bones, it was said, lay buried deep inside this wall, reinforcing fibres that increased its elasticity and solidity.

Embedded in this empire traversed by the Great Dragon under an ebony vault strewn with river pearls to represent the night sky, China's great rivers sparkled: Huáng Hé, the Yellow River; Cháng Jiāng, the Long River, whose name as inscribed on Western globes was the Yangtze Kiang; Méigōng Hé, the Mekong; Hēilong Jiāng, the Black Dragon River; and Zhū Jiān, the Pearl River, whose labyrinthine tangle of tributaries formed a watery net that snared every treasure reachable by ship, ferry or raft.

These and other rivers, major and minor, each thousands of miles long in the outside world, wound their way beneath the pavilion's ebony sky from the highest mountains, capped with mother-of-pearl glaciers, to the Yellow Sea and the South and East China Seas. But the silver gleam of the water, which seemed to reflect the light of an invisible sun hanging in the black sky, did not stem from fresh or salt water but solely from the hundreds of pounds of mercury with which the model-makers had flooded the riverbeds, the oceanic basins and the lakes. The lustre that made this empire magical was the lustre of mercury.

Paradoxically, it was Lockwood who remembered their first visit to the imperial model when they were debating and listing the materials that would be necessary to fulfil the Emperor's latest whim. Accompanied by a horde of distrustful secret-service officials and a few artisans and stonemasons who had helped build this landscape, the Englishmen had wandered for hours one boiling day along the boundaries of this empire which was so extensive that an awestruck walker like Merlin (who had gone ahead of his companions towards a distant defensive wall) was soon out of hailing distance.

One of the officials hurried after him and signalled politely for him to stay with the group, for whether it was the borders of reality or those of their model version, nobody was allowed to roam at their own discretion here.

Lockwood had eyes only for the mercury rivers and bodies of water during that visit. They appeared to be the only moving element of that sparkling landscape, a mysterious, metallic glow that the visitors' solemn footsteps barely brought to a quiver.

Lockwood thought back with horror to that morning in the workshop in London when a cat had slunk between his legs and tripped him up. He was carrying to his workbench a flask full of mercury destined to be installed in the great barometer of St Catherine's Lighthouse on the Isle of Wight . . . and even with a sidestep, he had been unable to keep his balance.

As well as innumerable shards of glass, on which he cut his feet, hands and even his forehead, the shattering a moment later sent mercury globules shooting in all directions, gleaming prey which not just one but three cats immediately pounced on—and not just cats. Abigail, a three-year-old girl at the time, who repeatedly delighted even the fine mechanics and goldsmiths at the manufactory and caused them to set down their tools, had been trying in vain to catch one of the cats until Lockwood stumbled and sprawled on the floor, but had settled after her initial shock at Lockwood's fall for the much more attainable silvery globules; and she was just about to put one of them in her mouth when Cox, who had been watching the accident from his drafting table, rushed towards his daughter with a cry of horror. She started to cry as he dashed the mercury from the little hand she had already raised to her mouth.

Shuiyín: Lockwood first heard the Chinese name for mercury on their visit beneath the pavilion's ebony vault because Kiang responded to Merlin's question about the effulgence of the rivers, lakes and seas by whispering the word over and over again as he frantically leafed through sheets of densely written English vocabulary. *Shuiyín*. Shuiyín.

And Lockwood once more heard Abigail's sobs in his ears and dared not look at Cox, who was standing some distance away, leaning against the edge of this model world, absorbed by the light reflecting on the waves of the Yangtze Kiang.

Yet a few days later, when talk during the morning's discussion of materials for the *perpetuum mobile* turned to obtaining mercury and Kiang was loath to mention the most obvious source, Lockwood said, The rivers, the streams! The South China Sea. How about the miniature landscape in the Black Pavilion? Let's drain the Empire.

ZHŌNG

The Clock

For the mandarins, generals, masters of ceremonies and even the tradesmen hired to maintain the walls, the golden beaked roofs or the lacquered floors, the greatest outrage perpetrated by these fine mechanics from England against the ancient rites of the court was that the foreigners' influence had caused some of China's greatest rivers to run dry.

The Huáng Hé, the Làn Cháng Jiāng and even the Hēilong Jiāng, the Black Dragon River, venerated as a direct link between gods, demons and humans—all dwindled by the day. Eunuchs ladled their silvery waves, more suggested than seen, into glass vases which they carried out of the Black Pavilion to the Englishmen's island among the swaying lotus leaves. In a move unintelligible to even his most intelligent and reasonable subjects, the Emperor had agreed that the mercury lakes and rivers, great and small, should be diverted to feed a machine that the court was coming to hate—a machine that was to point the way from order into timelessness!

With the draining of its great rivers, the model of the empire seemed to take on a graphic and ominous portent: the waning silvery lustre of its true-to-scale system of watery veins seemed to detract from the glory of the mountains, cities and fortresses made of alabaster, graphite, quartz sand and ironwood. Even the glister of the icy armour on the highest peaks (although these rose no higher than anthills inside the Black Pavilion) and the mirror-like seas risked being dulled.

And yet at first no one dared to voice, even in secret, what was on the minds of all those who had seen a major artery dwindle to a trickle, a river become a silver thread, and lakes, empty craters inside this pavilion. Had the foreigners bewitched His Sublime Majesty, or cast a spell on him with their needle-thin instruments and tools?

His Sublime Majesty gave permission for silver shavings to be strewn where rivers had once adorned the replica of his empire, filings that did not come close to creating the same vivacity as the liquid metal that would now be put to a perverted use as a component of a pointless machine. His Sublime Majesty permitted the greatest and holiest rivers to be emptied and carried to the quarters and lathes of a handful of mute foreigners, adding further fuel to the piles of gold, platinum, diamonds and precious gems that already fired their delusions.

Occasional pacifying voices among the initiated reminded people that the silver shavings would actually only be scattered there until a delayed delivery of mercury from Shànghǎi finally arrived, but to little effect. These foreigners were endangering, even flouting the summer peace. What the Englishmen were casting on His Sublime Majesty was an evil spell—or a curse that perhaps only their blood could expunge.

Cox, Merlin, Lockwood and even Kiang had no inkling of the storm of hostile thoughts brewing silently and imperceptibly behind expressionless faces whenever one of them appeared and requested an errand or a favour.

Cox interpreted the fact that the Emperor himself had decreed that the mercury from the Black Pavilion be brought to the Englishmen so that work on the *Timeless Clock* (this was how His Sublime Majesty had cheerfully christened this latest project in two mandarins' presence) might begin without delay as a sign that Qiánlóng had never been more favourably disposed towards him and his companions than in those late summer days.

But in Jehol's streets and alleys, bathed in the golden glow of the roofs, people here and there occasionally whispered, in secret places or behind magnificent ante-lope-parchment fans decorated with poems, about *The Play of the Eyes*—a calendar motto from the Tang dynasty that featured as a calligraphy in many a master of ceremony's books of protocol. One day someone even daubed the motto in blood-red paint on a palace wall. (But even after several weeks of secret-service investigations and the torturing of several suspects, two of whom did not survive their interrogation, the identity of its author had still not come to light.)

Even an emperor, the bloody message read one grey morning after a stormy night in characters as big as the figures in a shadow play on the gilded back wall of the Pavilion of Windless Days:

> *Even an emperor*
> *speaks with only one voice,*
> *sees with only two eyes,*
> *hears with only two ears.*
> *His court, however,*
> *speaks and whispers*
> *with a thousand voices,*
> *sees with a thousand eyes,*
> *hears with a thousand ears*
> *and does with a thousand hands*
> *what a sea of eyes*
> *cannot see*
> *if every eyelid shuts*

*in the face
of what must be done.*

On sunny days, when the air in the workshop in the Pavilion of the Four Bridges sparkled with the light reflected by the waves of the lake, Cox felt almost carefree for the first time since he had arrived in Qiánlóng's empire. The Emperor was providing them with all the necessary means to realize a mechanical fantasy so many European workshops had dreamt of in vain. The initial trials, using a series of elaborate flasks supplied to his specifications by glassblowers in the province of Ānhuī, demonstrated that a single one of these vessels, filled with mercury, could supply an abundance of energy due to the variations in pressure over the course of a day. The first construction drafts and calculations showed that this glut might even cause problems: what would prevent a chain from eventually tearing as this incredible power pulled a movement's brass or gold weight higher and higher?

Merlin: it was Jacob Merlin, a virtuoso when it came to mechanics and the delicate refinement of all its components, who within a week came up with a relief mechanism that involved the winding wheel sliding out of the teething when the tension got too great, and the wheel was gently reunited with the freewheeling, still-whispering cogs when fleeing time and the pull of gravity made the weight sink back to earth; sink back to earth, out of whose stony darkness everything was constantly striving up and up towards the circling orbs, the glittering stars, the light.

Jacob Merlin. Since the day of the imagined pirate attack on the *Sirius*, when he had hugged Cox, he sometimes laid a hand on the master's arm, once even on his shoulder, to show his admiration or particular agreement. And Cox, who was regarded as untouchable even by his close friends and the privileged foremen among the gold- and silversmiths in his manufactories, and who sometimes shied away from shaking the outstretched hand of a guest or even a noble-born client, did not brush Merlin's hand away but stood motionless for a few heartbeats. Just stood there until he felt the warmth of Merlin's palm through his clothes.

As if this light-flooded workshop in the middle of an expansive lotus pond deep in the Chinese interior was the only possible place to realize the idea that mercury, expanded and stirred by rising and falling air pressure, could drive a cog, and the cog a shaft, and the shaft the wheel train of a clock, the work on the Timeless Clock weighed lightly on Cox, as lightly as a feather, almost like a game in which there was everything to gain and nothing to lose.

It was not just thoughts and calculations regarding the construction but also the most diverse materials that dove-tailed perfectly, as if nothing, nothing at all, had happened, apart from that the time had come—the time when the implementation of a long and vainly sought-after principle would force its way into the world as unstoppably as an embryo, a child . . . No, no; it was more beautiful, more urgent, for unlike the birth of a human being, the realization of a mechanical idea could be grasped in its full complexity, could be controlled and was not a mystery, not a miracle like a child whose dying began, in truth, with its very first breath.

This clock, though; this clock had only one direction of travel, and anyone who wished to turn the moments it measured into striking hours and seconds would start the journey into eternity long before his death.

Transmission gearing, screws and escape wheels, one barrel and another, anchor and verge escapements and a virtually airtight, octagonal glass case to protect it from the all-grinding dust, platinum-set diamonds and rubies, whose surfaces could reduce the destructive friction between moving parts to insignificant levels . . . Even if it were possible to convert all his deliberations into components, it sometimes seemed to Cox as if all the parts made from wood, glass, a wide range of metals and gemstones were moving and revolving around one another not in a mechanical process but, ultimately resonating, as if in an alchemist's kitchen, in an organic swirl from which, some day, everlasting youth, the philosopher's stone or eternity was bound to tumble like a river pebble borne by an overwhelming and irreversible current.

In his unspoken triumph at the convergence of his own longings and fantasies with the Emperor of China's dreams, Cox did not notice that, although the days were still long and often summery, the twittering of the birds was becoming less varied, and it was growing darker and quieter.

Some of the whispering voices at court, which had started as imperceptibly as the first gentle draughts and breezes preceding a storm—voices which even Kiang could not hear—were calling for these Western sorcerers to be driven out or even killed. These accursed long-noses had merely disguised themselves as jewellers and goldsmiths when they were really spies endowed with magic powers, enemies of the Empire capable of confounding even the soul and heart of an Emperor who enjoyed both his people's and the heavens' favours.

Even though Kiang's confidants in the court were careful not to let him in on certain rumours and suspicions, the translator, who had been cheerful and brimming with conversation only a few weeks previously, grew increasingly taciturn under the weight of his premonitions. He was the first to rise each morning and whisper instructions to two eunuchs about the breakfast preparations or their subsequent tasks for the day, but would then answer none of Merlin and Cox's concerned enquiries regarding his apparently clouded, and therefore surely passing, mood.

Only when Merlin laid out the construction plans for the Timeless Clock before Kiang, as he presumed that the translator would convey all the events and discussions to the secret service and therefore wished to procure him a triumph, a scrap of significant information, did Kiang, their unspeaking, omnipresent shadow no less, try to warn the English clockmakers with hitherto unknown passion about the consequences of what they were building.

Suicide! It was suicide to build a clock for all eternity, a clock that chimed the hours from the centre of time out into timelessness. Did the Englishmen not realize that the Lord of Ten Thousand Years not only reigned over time but *was* time? That not only Qiánlóng's life but the whole of time began with him and ended with him? Every dimension of size and area and space, every name, every creation legend and scientific and philosophical truth that served to explain, measure, name or enhance the world would have to be re-ordained, re-defined, re-told when the Lord of Ten Thousand Years died. The end of an emperor of China spelt the end of the world.

And a clock such as the one the Englishmen planned to create here in the peace and quiet of the summer palace, a clock that would outdo the Emperor, continuing to turn beyond his lifetime and ultimately consigning even him to a mere bit part in a higher course of time, must necessarily stake a claim to being more enduring and greater than him! More enduring than the Lord of Time, reducing him to a mortal, just one among many. And this sorcery transformed everything he ruled over, everything he possessed, everything that delighted him, everything he loved into worthless flotsam on a pretend river of silver shavings.

Did the English guests truly believe that His Sublime Majesty or his court would countenance such humiliation, such sacrilege?

As Kiang whipped himself into a confused state of fear and outrage, Cox looked out at the wind-tattered lotus flowers beyond his window. Wild gusts, rasping the surface of the lake from all directions, chased hundreds of petals the colour of cyclamens and Christmas roses like fleets of toy ships across water that had only seconds earlier been as smooth as glass, beaching them on sandy patches of bank against insurmountable barriers of taproots and driftwood.

From where these petals had piled up, a child at play would no doubt have been able to catch the screams of seafarers who had foundered along with their lotus-petal boats, hear the tiny voices of the irretrievable sailors under the slapping tiny sails as they tried to defend themselves against beachcombers including prowling, heavily armoured beetles, low-darting dragonflies and short-sighted ornamental fish which mistook an airborne seed drifting down out of a rain-filled sky for an unsuspecting insect and made a daring, leaping snap for it, only to fall back into the open mouths of invincible predatory fish lurking just below the surface.

Kiang went on speaking. Yet all Cox could hear were the tiny voices and shrill mayday cries of the seafarers stranded on their lotus-petal ships as they fought for their lives; Abigail would surely have seen and heard them too.

By now the summer was meandering to its end. The advent of stormy north-easterly winds and the turning of the leaves brought messengers practically every day from the Forbidden City with missives that seemed to be connected to an imminent departure and the proclamation of autumn.

On one of these days, a rainy day, eunuchs lit fires not only in the living quarters but for the first time also in the workshop. But although it grew stuffy and hot at the lathes when the sun once more broke through the clouds after a heavy shower and glittered on the now petal-free surface of the pond, Cox began to shiver. The alternation of sunny spells and sudden cold showers had sent the air pressure rocketing up and then plummeting down again, causing such movement in the flasks made by the glass-blowers of Ānhuī that he at last felt confirmed in his belief that these dynamics represented perhaps the sole source of energy for a mechanism that, once set in motion, would never cease.

During that period, however, the inventor, once more enveloped in his old sadness, barely referred to his timepiece—at least in his conversations with Merlin and Lockwood—by the name the Emperor had bestowed on it—the Timeless Clock—but by a mocking nickname or pet name Merlin had coined in an attempt to raise his master's spirits: *Clox.*

Clox. Could there be a more natural combination than that of a word inspired by the sound of a chiming bell and the name of the creator of this unique and peerless clock?

Seventy rubies, by Merlin's estimates, must be inserted into this piece and more than fifty diamonds and sapphires. The crown-glass case, into which Wàn lǐ cháng chéng, the Great Wall, the Ten-Thousand-Times-Unimaginably-Long Wall, was to be etched as an opaque dragon armed with battlements and beacon-towers, would not conceal as other clock cases did (most of them in order to hide the ungainliness of their design) but reveal all the secrets of its construction. It must *show* everything: the elegant mercury-filled flasks, the silver-plated gimbal mountings, the golden weights and pivot arms, the latches chased with endless garlands of lotus and bamboo leaves, and ratchet wheels made of cobweb-fine polished brass . . . And on the base of pitch-black Tibetan granite on which the head-high octagonal pillar rested, glass-cutters were to engrave a poem which the Emperor would write one future morning: words never pronounced nor heard before this clock's construction, words that would become present and past with the first hour chime of this clock—future poetry.

The engraving would be filled with platinum to create the impression of writing that had been painted in the dark with a calligraphy brush dipped in moonlight.

Maintenance-free, requiring no lubricants, left to its own devices and protected from even dust's corrosive grind by its octagonal cloak of glass, this clock's cog wheels would revolve into the farthest future, go on turning for eons and eons until a time when what had recently seemed great, impressive and invincible would crumble into its basic components while the principle of this work would retain its significance, and therefore its beauty, until the nameless end of everything—including one's loved ones, all shelter, all space, even time itself.

JING GÀO

A Warning

The Almighty One had ordered summer not to end. And summer obeyed. Although a fine drizzle sometimes set in for several days and the now-leaden light caused by low-hanging clouds stole the lustre from Jehol's roofs; although the long gingko-lined avenue linking seven pavilions, which its planners had imagined as a representation of a dragon's sinuous gait, was already beginning to lose its autumnal saffron hue and the crowns of the other trees that had grown concurrently with Jehol's walls were already bare; and although the deep, night-like blue of the Mongolian sky appeared rarely and only as narrow strips or blurry patches among the marching clouds; still, numb-fingered watercolourists had seized the opportunity on three days to paint bamboo glittering with needles of frost while candle flames warmed the little dishes in which they mixed their paints to prevent the water from freezing.

Yet, despite regular couriers from the Forbidden City, there were no further signs that the Lord of Ten Thousand Years would allow autumn to be proclaimed, announcing at last that preparations for the return to the heart of the empire could start in the stables, archives, armouries and clock collections. Even if the pleasure gardens lay cold in the fog and the rose-breeders crouched shivering beside withered bushes whose sole remaining decorations were mouldering rosehips, it was and remained summer, for the Lord of Ten Thousand Years refused to let time pass. The English masters' work must be completed here in Jehol, in the summer residence where there was only one season. Only then could a new season begin. For in Běijīng, the Englishmen had told one of the Emperor's grand secretaries, who had come to the workshop along with more than a dozen officials to draw up a schedule; in Běijīng, a large part of the work would have to start again from scratch—the piece was too well balanced, too delicate and as hard as a mountain, a lake or a cloud to transport, they had said, and must therefore be completed here and now or not until the next summer. Or—this was another possibility—they could dismantle the clock into its component parts and have them taken to the Forbidden City for reassembly. But not only would that be a huge waste of time, it would also mean reversing the course of time, and a new beginning.

Even though barely any inhabitants of Jehol, other than officials, had ever laid eyes on the *monster*, by now everyone who enquired knew that this endless summer could only be attributed to the machine that was growing beneath the Englishmen's hands and tools, a ghoul in the pavilion with the four footbridges that no priest, no curse and no counter-spell could control, and that was becoming increasingly uncanny.

Yet since it was not only the clock's glittering mass that grew but also the Emperor's delight in its exotic movement, its cog wheels, chains and glass cylinders shimmering with mercury, the court no longer dared so much as to whisper its thoughts. How easy it was for a whisperer's life to come to ruin after a supposedly sympathetic listener had filed a report to an officer the same day, whereas the witness's career would leap up into the highest spheres of reflected imperial glory.

Ever since the secret service had interrogated those suspected of daubing the walls of the Pavilion of Windless Days and two men had been tortured to death, thereby breaking the law stipulating that normal jurisdiction, all penalties and sentences were to be suspended until the return to the Forbidden City, no longer could a disgraced whisperer hope for his torment or execution to be deferred. No signal had come from the Emperor's shadow to countermand these altered circumstances.

Qiánlóng had passed the pavilion with the four foot-bridges during a two-day ritual in the course of which he and a large cortege had visited three temples dedicated to the divinities of a natural world sapped by the intensity and length of the summer days, but he had not entered the workshop, opting instead to have reports delivered to him in a curious chant by a correspondent who hovered on the threshold; yes, he really did have a report *sung* to him about what was to be seen at the workbenches, along with the answers the English guests had given to the questions called into the pavilion from that same threshold.

The summer went on, but it grew cold. Many of the pavilions and quarters built for a season filled with warmth and hours of sunshine had no heating, and blankets and furs were scarce in the warehouses. Anyone not sweating over his work froze. Tower furnaces glowed in the mandarins' chambers, as, every night, did fireplace surrounds cast to resemble gaping dragon mouths. But still this accursed summer would not end.

As if imprisoned by the hostile atmosphere, the English guests only left their pavilion when a rite marking the rising or setting of seasonal constellations or a ceremony in honour of a river god required their presence. The Englishmen had been invited to such ceremonies since they had begun their latest work, but they regarded this privilege as an irksome chore; actually, what kept them from going was their work which was progressing at an effortless pace.

As if the Emperor's joy and, yes, enthusiasm had gripped every one of them in a different way, Cox, Merlin and even Lockwood spent sleepless nights thinking of a machine to which they now only referred—in contrast to their previous derogatory nicknames for it, and in contrast above all to the many superstitious terms the court employed for the thing growing in their workshop—as *the Clock*.

The Clock. Did this monstrous mechanism, based on the movement wrung from an apparently living, lethal, liquid metal by the weight of the air, and whose endless operations offered a glimpse of eternity, bear any relation to the simple rattleboxes that merely struck the hour, woke a shepherd or made a bell tinkle?

The Emperor had tried one early morning to pen a poem about this timepiece (Qiánlóng later revealed this secret to a grand secretary who was making a list of his wishes regarding the machine). He had wasted half the morning on this attempted ode and ended up burning the sheet of rice paper with the calligraphy on it a brazier. The English guests' work should and would not be disturbed under any circumstances, but that was precisely what might happen if a poem—even a poem by the Almighty One—attempted to describe a nascent creation with inadequate, powerless words.

Kiang was still the only one in the Pavilion of the Four Bridges who was convinced that this clock might pose a threat to its constructors—and not just because of the toxicity of the hundredweights of mercury at its core. The English guests had not taken his warning seriously, discounting it on the assumption that the translator merely wanted their work to be interrupted so that the royal household (and he himself) might return to the long-awaited luxury of the Forbidden City.

Yet the days were full of ill omens. A blundering whelp, the palace puppy of a watercolourist dispatched by His Sublime Majesty to record developments in the workshop, had perished in hideous pain. The puppy had chased after the mercury globules rolling in all directions when a glass cylinder burst (as if in an ominous repetition of the accident that had occurred during the construction of a barometer in Shoe Lane), had swallowed some of them and then whimpered in pain until its death two days later. The painter, another eunuch, who had cherished the puppy like a child and did everything he could to save it, pinned the blame for his loss on the English sorcerers: they had contaminated his darling with their machine's poison.

Although a painter who enjoyed His Supreme Majesty's trust was powerful enough to harm anyone at court, this time the magnificence of the clock stifled any malicious slander. The Senior Grand Secretariat simply issued an order to compensate the watercolourist with another puppy from the same litter (for which a Manchurian provincial governor demanded a fortune until he was told that the puppy was for the court). No, even highly toxic mercury was a lesser—far lesser—danger than the true threat emanating from this clock's mechanism.

You're so silent, Cox asked the translator at the end of a particularly satisfying day's work because Kiang had said nothing for the whole afternoon, answering two questions about the Chinese name for a mechanical component with the words, *Don't know, I don't know, I'll look it up*. What's on your mind?

Cox, taciturn Master Cox, whose companions some-times got the impression during this period that work on this clock was breathing new life into him; this taciturn Cox had never before asked any of them or Kiang what was on their minds.

As if he had been waiting for this spell-breaking ques-tion, Kiang said quietly but unhesitatingly: You still don't understand what you're doing. Your work can kill you. You don't know what you're doing. It will kill you.

Although Kiang had whispered this, the companions at their workbenches fell as silent as they would have after the words of a master of ceremonies or a mandarin demanding *silence*. And even as Kiang started to repeat the warning he had droned out some weeks previously about the Timeless Clock in a monologue unbroken by any questions, the buzzing of a weary fly taking shelter from the coming frosts seemed louder than his imploring words.

The English guests still believed that they were fulfilling a great wish for the Emperor, but they were in fact screwing and slicing, sawing and sanding a gallows for themselves, said Kiang. They wanted to build a Timeless Clock for the Lord of Ten Thousand Years. Had they still not understood why Qiánlóng was so attached to clocks and chronometers? Did they still not know that the Emperor was the only person in his almost-boundless realm who was allowed to *play* with clocks, with time? Anyone who even contemplated such a clock must know that he was elevating himself above the sovereign by creating a mechanical replica of his power over time. Yet nobody and nothing was permitted to elevate itself, ever, above the Lord of Ten Thousand Years, with the possible exception of the sun, with the possible exception of the stars, but definitely no living human being.

Anyone attempting to soar to such heights, said Kiang, would at some point realize that up there, high above, there was room only for the Unique One, and that anyone else could expect nothing but death. The creators of a machine such as the one rising to ever-greater heights in the Pavilion of the Four Bridges could count on only one outcome to their toil: the final touches and its completion would spell their final hour. For the Ruler of China and the world must be alone with the course of his time, utterly alone, so that he might extend his power to the realms of the stars and of all light. But triumphs such as this must be, and must remain, indivisible.

Kiang had walked over to the eight-sided pillar of glass which was to keep the structure of the Timeless Clock safe from draughts and the grating dust, but he seemed to be contemplating his own reflection rather than the mechanism.

What was the man talking about? What was the translator talking about? Who were screwing and sawing a gallows for themselves?

You don't believe that yourself, said Merlin, tossing Kiang, as if in response to a joke, a brass cog he had just removed from the vice so unexpectedly that, although Kiang instinctively stretched out his hand to catch the cog, he couldn't grasp it and it fell to the floor.

What was this man talking about?

Had Kiang not noticed that the Emperor had come to inspect this workshop three times, three times! since work had commenced on the clock—once with a large, ceremonial retinue, once with a smaller one and then with a still smaller one—and even asked questions, the questions of a connoisseur, the questions of a clockmaker, which he, Kiang, had translated on his knees? Had the translator not realized that the Emperor was extending the summer, by week after week, indeed by months, in order to await and encourage the completion of a mechanical marvel of a kind never built before?

The impossibility of looking the Emperor in the eye, or at his face as he was enquiring and speaking, should have meant that whatever he said stuck more firmly in one's mind. However, Kiang had obviously forgotten what he himself had said with such awe and admiration: never before had Qiánlóng addressed a question to a craftsman nor even approached a place where work was being done, a workshop; yet he had visited the Englishmen's workshop again and again!

What rot the translator was talking.

Would a ruler, even a divine ruler, who was arranging his own plans around the work of three clockmakers from England, and who fixed the heart and head of his empire in Mongolia for this period, ultimately banish from time the creators of a wonder to whom he had hitherto shown so many signs of his gratitude? Would he do them harm or kill them?

Was it not rather fear speaking from Kiang, fear that he himself was becoming expendable and was going to lose his right to live? Had the Emperor, on his last visit, not brought along an Italian cartographer who, as part of the imperial entourage, had listened carefully but had several times corrected Kiang's translation and, at a sign from the Emperor, rendered Cox's answers into His Sublime Majesty's language?

And who was eventually to maintain the clock, said Merlin, when its creators, their work done, had to depart this life? Who would recalibrate the thing after long transport, after the journey back to Běijīng, after an earthquake, a thunderstorm with barometric capers or just a trivial problem?

This clock, said Cox, interrupting Merlin's tirade, this clock needs no one to maintain it and no one to recalibrate it. We are building it so it no longer needs humans. Not a single one. Not even us.

Not even us? Really? asked Merlin. All the better. The Almighty One will be glad. And we . . . we'll put our screwdrivers, pliers and hammers back in our toolbox and sail back to London, swaying in hammocks on the top deck of the *Sirius*, as rich men. Why should our client do away with even a single one of us? When has a clockmaker ever been dispatched into the afterlife for accomplishing his mission and setting in motion a commissioned piece ahead of time and *for* all time?

Kiang turned away from Merlin, shut his eyes and shook his head, as if refusing to believe that a person could prove so incapable of grasping something so undeniable and obvious.

Lockwood, who was busy inscribing an endlessly recurring series of alphas and omegas from the Greek alphabet on every link of a brass chain, did not seem sure whether he had just heard an exchange of banter or a genuine warning of mortal danger. He gave Cox a quizzical look, his mouth agape. But Cox did not say a word.

The next morning, the first snow fell in large flakes and had, within minutes, covered the muddy hoofmarks of two mounted messengers and their escort carrying scrolls to the Forbidden City in sealed leather canisters. In the Pavilion of the Four Bridges, work went on as on any other day. Pearls of frankincense, a gift from an Arab delegation, brought from Běijīng by couriers and presented to the Englishmen as a further token of the Emperor's favour, smouldered in the braziers. The crackling of the embers, the singing of smouldering frankincense and the muffled noises of delicate engineering work were the only sounds.

On days like this, when there were no conversations with suppliers or tradesmen to be had or lists of materials to translate, Kiang did not even visit the workshop but waited in his two rooms for whenever he might be required, occupying himself with reading or bamboo painting.

Does he just mean to scare us, or does he truly believe in his stupid blathering? said Merlin after sitting silently for a long time at his workbench on which the cog he had tossed and Kiang had dropped the day before now lay in a plywood box of rejected parts. What's the man talking about? Our own clock will toll for us?

Maybe he's right, said Cox.

Maybe he's right? Have you gone mad? asked Merlin.

Maybe, said Cox.

Over the following days, no one in the workshop mentioned Kiang's warning again. As the translator's services were still not required at this stage of the work, he appeared only when meals were being prepared before taking himself off to his rooms or strolling for hours in the bare gardens and grounds which, lacking walls or fences, were almost indistinguishable from the wilderness. Or he would read while he strode among the summer residence's pavilions and palaces, as meltwater dripped from their roofs. Soon the only snow in sight was on the tops of the highest hills.

The mandarins believed they could see with alarming clarity that the recent increase in the number of couriers arriving from the Forbidden City on exhausted mounts and leaving Jehol again after one night at most carried not Běijīng's splendours in their saddlebags, canisters and leather pouches but very much its influence and power, in order to make the summer residence the heart of the empire for an indeterminate length of time.

All the documents, letters, orders and decrees bore a summer's day and Jehol as their date and place of issue. Surely this summer would not last for ever. It should and could not last for ever, surely. But for now it seemed never-ending. Time stood still.

GǏNG KÈ

The Moment

The pavilions and palaces of the summer residence lay snow-bound and frosted in the windless air as the Lord of Ten Thousand Years set off on foot along a path that no ruler over the Middle Empire had ever trodden. On this wintry morning, when the air shimmered with tiny ice crystals transformed into glittering needles by a cold sun, Qiánlóng had spent an unusually long time, many hours, in his floating bed dangling from its silken plaits, wordlessly dismissing every document, every plea and every petition presented to him. No patronage. No tax relief. No promotions, concessions or commendations. No pardons, either. Death and all life's events should either follow their blind course, undirected by a decision from on high, or remain unchanged that day.

The Lord of Ten Thousand Years wished, upon getting out of his bed that swayed like a raft and pushing away two eunuchs who had proffered their bodies, as usual, as props or footstools at a chamberlain's whispered command, to waste not one more second on pleas and petitions. Neither would he tolerate that anyone help him to dress nor, as he left the pavilion, that his secretaries, his bodyguards, guardsmen or warriors accompany and protect him with that rigidly ordered cordon, the customary impenetrable human shield.

He had only sent for one of his mistresses, ordering her to wait for him by the *Pavilion of Cloud-Writing*. On an icy day such as this, a constant stream of misty plumes rose from the pool fed by steaming-hot river water lying like a jade-bordered mirror before that pavilion; it rose in bands, whorls and puffs that really did resemble fleeting ideographs and were interpreted as such by astrologers on certain days of the celestial calendar.

Alone. Completely alone. The Emperor had stepped out of his pavilion, the best protected and safest place in the world, alone. Without bodyguards, without an escort. Later, of course, and on the two days that followed, when there was no further snowfall, only a frost that made the snowy blanket glitter, one could see how this dazzling blanket had been trampled on the pavilion's leeward side— trampled by the boots of camouflaged, well-concealed armed men who had followed the Almighty One's path with disbelief from the hiding places to which they had been assigned by the highest-ranking officers and officials: His Sublime Majesty, on his own like any normal walker, a hiker in the snow. Anyone who saw him trudging along from a distance would have noticed nothing, none of the many eyes watching his progress with heightened vigilance from cover, none of the many clandestine guardians behind bushes and walls, standing shivering in their hiding places, anxious to remain invisible. The only person visible was a man draped in furs, walking across the pristine white expanses of the courts towards the drifting ideographs of steam above the Pavilion of Cloud-Writing.

In the shadow of a parasol pine burdened with snow at the halfway point, a woman in a sable-fur gown waited for him, wraithed in wisps of mist. Her crystallizing breath looked like a delicate imitation or a quotation of the cloud-writing drifting over the hot river water: Ān. The daintiest and sweetest of all the Emperor's cherished, dainty and sweet mistresses breathed here, waited here.

Although the Ruler of the World always searched for the most fitting description during the morning hours when he was inclined to poetry, the words *dainty* and *sweet* were nevertheless the words he used most frequently when thinking of this childlike woman, composing a line about her or running his fingers across her cheek, even in front of witnesses, as gently as if he must first check before every word he addressed to her that this creature was real and tangible and not just a supernatural apparition that would melt away and dissolve at a covetous gaze, let alone a touch. My dainty. My sweet. My beauty.

Ān did not like these and other trite pet names, but never omitted to react to them with a smile. The Emperor had exempted her from the obligatory kowtow when he summoned her. He even allowed her an act that would otherwise have carried the death penalty—to look into his eyes as grey as feldspar, in whose depths navy-blue inclusions were visible, which almost none of the Emperor's mistresses had ever glimpsed. And he permitted her to trace with the tip of her index finger the shape of his lips, which might at any second curl in judgement over the lives and fates not only of every one of his subjects but also of the whole world, until a sensual shudder elicited a strange, indeed crazed-sounding, high-pitched giggle from him.

Ān revered and admired this man who had raised her so high above any other woman in the empire. She was grateful to him and always responded to his demands out of gratitude and never fear. But she did not love him.

Qiánlóng had sunk his footsteps into the snow as if following a taut plumbline and stopped at some distance from the small retinue that had accompanied Ān to the meeting point and now prostrated themselves in the snow before the Ruler of the World. But he called to them—no, he said to them in the low tones of someone soliloquizing—that they were to disappear, erasing them from the white, snowy scene with a single, casual wave: all but one were to disappear, the dainty one, the sweet one, with whom a few heartbeats later he stood apparently alone on that winter's day.

Wrapped in their coats, the two of them advanced towards each other across this great white plain like two furry animals. Whether they touched, whispered something to each other or murmured greetings and pet names in incomprehensible animal voices was not visible, was not audible to the many eyes and ears concealed amid the glittering snow crystals.

Noiselessly, the distance between them narrowed. And then the Lord of the Horizons turned away from his warmly wrapped mistress as they passed, and continued his path through the untouched snow. And as if this were a well-rehearsed ritual, even in the snow, Ān followed him at a distance of three of her body-lengths, as prescribed in a *Catalogue of Steps* and binding even on His Sublime Majesty's wives and concubines. The Emperor's will and fancy alone could reduce this gap.

No observer could have heard if Qiánlóng had mentioned the destination of their walk together as he passed his beloved, but it was easy to see where the couple was heading: to the Timeless Clock. They were making for the Pavilion of the Four Bridges. The cloud-writing lay along the path to the English guests' house. The invisible eyes and ears followed the two of them in suspense and from ever-changing hiding places and ever-changing concealments they watched this unheard-of spectacle: the Emperor on foot. The Emperor like a farmer on the way to his snow-covered field, accompanied only by a woman, a concubine for whom his paces through the snow were slightly too long and who therefore occasionally stumbled as she followed him with uncertain steps.

Get down! Heads and weapons quickly pulled out of sight behind a snowdrift or a jutting wall, behind a tree trunk or shrub. Even if the walker paused, raised his head and listened out, if a pad of snow came loose in the morning sun and fell rustling from the branches, he was to have no inkling of his protectors whose vigilant, combat-ready presence in this barren whiteness only remained a secret because His Sublime Majesty's attention was focused more than anything on his lover. Warm from walking through the deep snow, she pushed back her fur hood and her long hair fell over her shoulders in shimmering metallic black cascades.

Laugh? Did she just laugh? Oh yes, almost all the anxiously ducking protectors had heard her laugh. She had tripped in the Emperor's footsteps and he had turned around, like any mortal to his wife, like any man, like any farmer, and she had fallen stumbling and laughing into his arms.

Followed by so many eyes and yet an apparently solitary couple in the snowy landscape, the two of them now tramped towards the English guests' house. Only a river gull sailing over the summer palace or a quivering falcon spying its prey far below could have seen how the couple were shadowed every step of their way by a flitting, sneaking, sometimes even crawling escort.

Disappear, the Emperor had said, disappear. For the mandarins who were responsible for the Almighty One's safety, however, that could only mean: Out of my sight! And now His Sublime Majesty might look in any direction and see no tracks, no irritating figure and nothing in any direction save wintry emptiness, snow-capped buildings and frosted wastes.

And no gull or falcon could be heard, only the occasional, silence-rending cry of a hungry crow and the muttering of the hot river which kept its banks green even in the depths of winter and brought purple and scarlet marsh flowers to bloom even on days of severe frost.

This scene of a couple flanked by a hidden retinue amid barren, wintry countryside seemed a fine illustration of something that had hardened into mysterious and irrefutable fact in recent weeks. Whenever and wherever talk turned to the Timeless Clock—whether it was described by a worried mandarin as a diabolical piece of sorcery, or construed as a wonder by eunuchs well versed in the maintenance of chimes and automata—the Emperor always wanted to be left alone to engage in a form of soliloquy with this creation. He wished to hear no judgements or opinions or assessments about a mechanism that was determining his life like no other, as this machine increasingly seemed a sign and symbol of his existence. It dominated mortal time as the Lord of Ten Thousand Years did. It struck its hours beyond the boundaries of the days and the years but did not require anyone to extend its running by further winding when its reserves had been exhausted; and if at some stage in the unconceivable future it ceased to chime, that did not spell the end of its life but the end of time itself.

As if Qiánlóng wished to recreate the empty expanse of awe, admiration and anxiety which court rules stipulated should surround his throne, his appearances and his every step around the Englishmen's work, the number of companions he tolerated on his visits steadily diminished until finally, on this winter's day, he granted this privilege to only one other person: the beautiful one, the dainty one, Ān.

Three times the Emperor had visited the Pavilion of the Four Bridges, and as if each one of these visits had not already caused enough of a stir, His Sublime Majesty now spoke to the English magician as if they were members of his family. He asked questions and allowed the addressees to answer from a standing position, not sprawling before him in the dust or on their knees. He protected only his countenance, refusing to revoke the ban on anyone, even the English guests, looking the Son of Heaven in the eye.

Already on the second of these visits he had demonstrated with a typically casual yet categorical gesture that he wished to be alone with this clockwork. Everyone, absolutely everyone, including the machine's constructors, was to leave the room containing the towering clock inside its octagonal glass column before he entered it. The clock should wait for the Lord of Ten Thousand Years in the same isolation as only one of his mistresses usually did.

How much longer? How much time until it was completed?

This question, which had never been put to Cox and his companions about any of the machines they had built at court, had been delivered after the third visit by a secretary dressed entirely in mandarin red, along with a gift from His Sublime Majesty—a fist-sized snail made of red gold. Kiang interpreted this as a sign of wealth and happiness, for only someone able to savour the luxury of slowness was able to entertain a dream of *possessing* that most precious good available to man: time.

So: how much time?

The Englishmen said, A few weeks.

How *many* weeks? The secretary returned the same day to request a number. His litter-bearers could be heard panting outside the open front door. The answer was obviously an urgent matter.

Six. Maybe only five if the new amalgamated glass cylinders for the clock's mercury heart were delivered as promised. However, given the prevailing snowy conditions, it might not be possible to keep that promise.

Yes, it would be. Every promise given to an imperial envoy, said the secretary, who insisted on waiting for a straight answer this time; every one of these promises was kept, even if the snow drifted higher than a house or flooded rivers transformed the land into sea and mountains into islands.

Neither Cox nor Merlin nor Lockwood saw or even guessed at the presence of the couple tramping towards the pavilion that morning—the fourth visit by the Ruler of Continents and Oceans.

Kiang had already had breakfast cleared away, and the two lackeys, having cooked and served in silent submission as every day, had vanished again. Another short, frenzied day of work appeared to pursue its unbroken course. Cox did not like working by the light of lanterns and wax candles and would therefore always declare the end of work before sundown. The timepiece was approaching completion and was already hardly distinguishable from the sketch that Cox had pinned to the eastern wall of the workshop alongside a sheet of paper inked with Chinese ideographs.

The Emperor's visits had always been announced by a messenger from the Grand Secretariat and awaited with palpitations. But this time the English guests were huddled quietly over their work—the glass cylinders needed remounting—when a stream of icy air from the corridor signalled that the door had either been opened or been forced ajar by a gust of wind. The gold-plated dragon's head that banged on the front door before each visit had not moved. The draught swept several papers from Cox's desk, and Kiang was hurrying to the door, cursing under his breath, when his sudden silence caused the English guests to glance up.

Cox was the only one to enjoy a clear view of the doorway between the corridor and the workshop from his chair, but there he saw nothing but Kiang's feet, as if the translator had fallen flat on his face in his rush to shut the door or to prevent an uninvited guest from disturbing their work. The rest of his body must have been pointing towards the front door, but it was hidden from sight in the dimly lit corridor.

Cox and his companions had spoken no more of this threat since Kiang's second warning that the creator of the Timeless Clock was elevating himself like a blasphemer above the Lord of Ten Thousand Years, and that the completion of his work would spell the end for him. Merlin occasionally mocked the courtiers' jealousy which they suspected rather than felt or suffered from inside the Pavilion of the Four Bridges, but he perceived malicious slander, easily rebutted, as the gravest danger.

An attack on the Emperor's guests within the walls of the summer residence, though? Such a crime, Merlin had said, would strike fear into countless members of the royal household that they might die under torture in the course of the secret service's investigations—if not here in Jehol, given the summer laws, then at a later date in the dungeons of Běijīng.

Although Cox appeared to have forgotten Kiang's warning, he remained secretly convinced that the translator was right, and this conviction grew with every workday that brought them closer to the completion of the work. The Emperor preferred to be left alone with his clock even now, so, after a timepiece like this, what more could the

Lord of Time or any other patron ask of an automaton-builder?

This glass column was the sum of all that the art of clock-making was capable of accomplishing, not only now but surely far into the future, everything Cox and his kind had dreamt of all their lives and which people were still dreaming about in parts of the world where they knew nothing of the triumph in Jehol: *perpetuum mobile.* If ever a mechanical work worthy of this title had been designed and built, then it was this column, which had glittered like an altar in a room adjoining the workshop at the Emperor's suggestion since his last visit.

Even though the physicists of England and China between them might object that this column did not enclose a self-contained system that, once set in motion, would run and run under its own power, but was, like a wound-up weight, reliant on rising and falling air pressure and hence did not deserve to be called a dream, they must be as aware as Cox that no entirely self-contained system could exist in this world and must therefore remain as out of reach of human hands as the throne of a god.

However, this clock, which could tick off and display every hour of the life and death of its creators and their off-spring far into the future without further human intervention, came as close to a mechanical wonder as any human invention to date. And compared with the fleeting length of organic life, its longevity was a better approximation of the notion of eternity than all the heroes and saints worshipped today, then toppled from their pedestals, pulverized with pickaxes or incinerated in a ball of fire tomorrow.

But even if this clock threatened his life and ultimately claimed it, Cox was prepared and impelled to complete it without reviewing the dangers with his companions. He had continually tried to assuage his forebodings in recent weeks with the thought that if the threat were real, then he was its only target, not Merlin and not Lockwood. After all, from a spy's standpoint, neither of them could be judged capable of building a clock like this and could therefore not interfere with a Lord of Time's claim to be its sole possessor. For him, though, the two men were indispensable; their master's dream could not be realized without them. Why then should he worry his assistants with premonitions whose validity they already doubted?

The clock. *His* clock. The timepiece must be finished at all cost. Not only because something that had long been a dream was finally coming true, and not because it was the Emperor of China's desire, but because the longings that bound this column to its creator had been joined, in Jehol, where time had slowed down and now ground to a halt, by another, still-greater hope.

While he and his companions in the Pavilion of the Four Bridges took the final steps towards their goal, at the other end of the world, in a wood-panelled room in London's Shoe Lane, his beloved wife Faye, who had been struck dumb after Abigail's death, would recover her speech and return to her senses and to him. As in a synchronically coupled mechanism, every spring and every screw turned in the Pavilion of the Four Bridges would bring back one syllable, then a word, then a sentence, which she would first pronounce in a whisper, then as clearly and audibly as all the many pet names with which she had regaled him such an infinitely-long-but-neverforgotten time ago.

Alister Cox believed that he was connected to his far-away wife by these gears and, more so, by the clock's cylinders, created by anonymous glassblowers in Ānhuī, in which the metal meniscus of mercury from China's greatest rivers rose and fell imperceptibly over the course of a day, like a restless heart quivering with love. Yes, when he surrendered and listened excitedly to the sounds of the mechanical tests, he began to hear, above the whispering of the mechanism, Faye breaking her silence, heard her voice so clearly that he was beginning to mouth answers when she asked something and hasty questions to stop her from falling silent again. Merlin and Lockwood occasionally looked up in surprise from their lathes: their master was talking to himself.

Cox had risen from his chair and, braving the stream of cold air, walked towards the door to see to Kiang who had obviously tripped and whose feet were still motionless in the doorway. The sight of the Emperor stopped him in his tracks and forced him to his knees.

Qiánlóng wordlessly stepped across the threshold, clumps of snow clinging to his embroidered boots and snow crystals to his pearl-studded snow-leopardskin coat and a hat crafted from the same fur. Cox could not see the Emperor's mistress following one or two breaths behind, for he had bowed his head and shut his eyes to avoid the crime of a forbidden glance.

Merlin and Lockwood too had dropped to their knees, pressed their foreheads to the floor and felt the metal filings of their day's work again, for even though, much to his attendants' ire, they had been granted permission during the Son of Heaven's previous visits to rise and answer his questions from a standing position—and although he had treated them as companions on the bank of the hot river—this, like any other favour, was only ever valid for a moment. Yesterday's begrudged, outrageous privilege might be today's fateful, life-threatening error. There were no precedents to fall back on in an encounter with the Ruler of the World.

Cox now heard the Emperor's quiet, deep voice and, after a few seconds of silence, Kiang saying, You are to stand up. You have nothing to fear.

Cox got hesitantly to his feet with his head bent and his eyes still shut. He didn't know if Merlin and Lockwood were doing the same and could not see who was coming towards him either when Kiang, after another word from the Emperor, said in a quivering voice, obviously still lying prone in the chilly corridor: Master Cox, you are to open your eyes. The Son of Heaven wishes to see your eyes.

Before Cox could work out whether this meant that he should now keep his head bowed and only open his eyes, or if the Emperor really had commanded his English guests to look at him, he caught a wonderfully aromatic fragrance, a perfume of a kind that even the wives of his richest clients had never sent wafting his way; an aroma that conjured inside his head a vision of a garden in which a gentle breeze mingled the scents of various flowers and carried them out into an odourless, colourless wasteland.

His closed eyes allowed him, even in the Emperor's presence, to be alone with his thoughts for at least a few breaths longer, and that complex aroma brought to his mind a babbling brook, a stream meandering through the garden. And then he saw Abigail. Abigail crouching by the shallows, tossing into the rippling waters woodchips that became ships, fishes, floundering dwarves and who knew what else. She was playing. And beside her sat Faye.

Cox was so intoxicated by this heady fragrance that he wanted to stay where he was, even against the will of the Ruler of the World—stay for ever in the shelter of his closed eyes, behind a curtain pulsing with his own blood, where everything was conceivable and dreamable, and could not be refuted by the sight of reality.

Suddenly, silky hands touched his eyebrows as delicately as if their lines must first be traced, their arches verified, before the hands ran along the sweep of the eyebrows and down over his temples, and fragrant fingertips caressed his shut lids, as one caresses the face of a corpse when closing its eyes.

But these hands . . . these hands sought to fetch him back from the darkness, back to life. These hands, these fingers intended to open his eyes at the Emperor's command. No sooner had they touched his eyelids as gently as a kiss than Cox obeyed—and opened his eyes at last. And saw not the Emperor before him but the radiant features of Ān, the most untouchable and forbidden woman in the whole empire. It was forbidden to touch not just her hand but even the hem of her robe, and even more forbidden were any thoughts to which her beauty might mislead a man. When Ān appeared for ceremonial receptions at the Almighty One's side, in the company of some of his other wives and concubines, mind- and face-readers had to delve into every face turned her way. What they read there might cost the beautiful one, the dainty one's secret suitor his office and send him to a dungeon or the scaffold.

Ān had lowered her arms, but she was still standing close to Cox, mesmerizing him by her sight and her scent, when Qiánlóng signalled to Kiang that he and the two other Englishmen should get up and precede him into the adjacent room where the column awaited. They were to answer a number of questions there. The Emperor stepped up behind Ān and put his hands over her eyes as in a children's game or as if he wished to release Cox from the spell of her sight.

But Cox was far away. Now he saw his garden even when his eyes were open, only this time Ān was sitting at the water's edge with Faye and Abigail, each as longed for, as beloved and as unattainable as the other. Then something took hold of him, a convulsion he might have sensed at Abigail's birth or the first time he lay in Faye's arms. He felt that this one moment face to face with the Emperor and his lover was no longer anchored in time but was, instead, without beginning or end, much shorter than the flare of a meteorite and yet as overflowing as eternity—a moment no clock could measure, as apparently unexpandable as a glittering pinprick in the heavens billions of years from the Earth.

Maybe every person was promised this light but none could ever claim it for himself, and it roved instead over heads and hearts, pausing for an incalculable moment before moving on. And anyone who hoped that this glimmer, this glow might attach itself for ever to a lover, a loved one, was merely following a path through a maze at whose end there were nothing but ashes.

But wasn't everyone upon whom this glow fell for one magical moment bound to another person for one beat of eternity as if for ever? Bound and filled with the certainty that everything in a human lifetime worthy of the name of love was now fulfilled. Everything, thought Cox; everything. And suddenly he sensed that this overflowing instant was the quintessence of time and, encased within it, as if trapped in amber, the presence of his silent and dead darlings coexisted with his desire for this untouchable, unattainable woman who stood smiling before him in the wintry light. The feeling that took hold of him now was stronger than any law, stronger than any fear of a sovereign, stronger even than the fear of death.

And so, before the eyes of the lover of the man who claimed to be the Lord of Heaven and Earth, he sank to his knees for a second time, unaware that he was weeping.

GŪ DŪ QÍU BÀI

The Invincible One

Could an unquenchable, overpowering desire . . . could tears beat back the commander-in-chief of five hundred thousand men, one hundred and fifty thousand horsemen and seven hundred warships?

When Cox opened his eyes, still on his knees, he saw only his concerned companions before him and, at a respectful distance, Kiang. The translator also clearly regarded tears as something of which one should be as wary of as molten iron. The Emperor had vanished, and the only reminder of his lover was a lingering residue of the fragrance that had transported Cox through time and space, deep into his yearnings and memories.

None of it? Was it true that Cox had witnessed none of what had occurred before his eyes? The Emperor had turned away without a word, Merlin said, and stepped out into the snow without a single glance at the column in the chamber. Nor had he asked any of his intended questions. The beauty in furs even tried, as she wordlessly followed him, to close the front door behind her like a good girl, but the wind had by then blown several handfuls of snow over the threshold. She gave up so as not to lose her master and disappeared in the Almighty One's footsteps.

In the first few weeks after this visit—weeks of warm weather when torrents of meltwater roared down from the mountains to the valley, lowering the temperature of the hot river with their chill and diminishing the quantity of steam characters and cloud-writing—no more signs came from the inner circles of power. No mandarins came, no secretaries, no news bearing the imperial seal or any of the long questionnaires about the Timeless Clock which they were always required to fill out on their knees.

Even to his guests from England, objects of the court's animosity and envy, Qiánlóng seemed to slip away once more into those remote, inaccessible realms where he resided, only ever assumed, never visible to his other subjects, like a divinity in whom one could believe but of whose existence splendid temples and palaces and merciless priests were the only evidence.

Cox had no doubt that Kiang's prophecies would be fulfilled once the final touches had been put to the clock. His patron would eliminate him and perhaps his companions too, because mortals had no place beside this timepiece. But he said nothing: not a word to Merlin and Lockwood who couldn't understand why, after so many months of urgent work and an obsession with time-saving, their master now wished to make a superfluous improvement here and add some new ornamentation there.

Embellishments! Why this procrastination? It was clear that the clock was ready. Or as good as ready. The fact that His Sublime Majesty had not reappeared since his last visit, after the master had prostrated himself before the lady-in-waiting in furs, meant that he had long been confident that his wish was being executed to his satisfaction and merely awaited news of its completion. Yet now of all times Alister Cox began to drag his feet.

Penelope, said Merlin to Cox over breakfast one morning. Do you remember Penelope?

Cox and Merlin had built a large, incredibly heavy table clock for the Edinburgh-born heiress of a Scottish textile factory—that was the year after founding their joint enterprise. A silver-plated model of a loom. They had named the automaton after Penelope, the unwavering

Spartan princess and faithful wife of the unfaithful wanderer Odysseus. Penelope had continued to weave a burial shroud for her father-in-law Laertes to keep at bay the suitors who beset her throughout the years her husband spent wading through blood in Troy and other distant lands, and to see which of them should succeed the lost hero on the throne of Ithaca—and in his wife's bed.

Time, Penelope had said, she needed time. She would make her decision only when the burial shroud was finished. But secretly, night after night, she unravelled her day's work to buy time—until one day she was betrayed by a maid who was later hanged for her crime.

To the ticking of its escapement and with a regular jerking motion, the automaton in Edinburgh had pushed out a carpet woven from threads of copper, gold and silver, a glittering kilim that was finished at every full moon but which the loom then swallowed up and unravelled, row by row, so that by the next new moon it had disappeared entirely. Then the automatic weaving would begin all over again.

Are you modelling yourself on our Penelope, Merlin asked again. Leaving his bamboo-shoot soup to go cold in its near-translucent porcelain bowl, Cox had insisted that the rubies from the Malay archipelago used as jewel bearings be replaced by diamonds from the Khmer empire. He had also reeled off a list of cog wheels that he doubted would see out even two of the coming centuries and wondered whether to replace them with an alloy of similar hardness and elasticity to Damascus steel.

The Emperor would surely understand, even if this meant prolonging the work a little further into the future. Had he not verified with his own eyes that nothing stood in the way of the work, and that its completion was only a matter of a not-easily-determined-yet-certainly-short span of time? After all, mechanically speaking, the path to their goal led through uncharted territory.

Yet whatever the arguments, like the Queen of Ithaca besieged by her suitors, Cox could neither stop time nor drag out the completion of the work for an indeterminate period or even for ever. And who knows, perhaps Kiang was already playing the role of the treacherous maid, informing the secret services of the undeniable fact that the English master was sabotaging the accomplishment of his own work.

Jehol was already regarded in both military and diplomatic circles as the new capital of the empire when an envoy from the Emperor unexpectedly appeared in the Pavilion of the Four Bridges one early spring day, and they were enjoined to finally list the reasons for the delay in their work, which Kiang noted down.

Disrupted, disharmonious trial runs had made it necessary, Cox dictated as his companions looked on in astonishment, to replace unexpectedly fragile materials with more durable ones. Glass cylinders also needed exchanging in order to increase the surface area of the mercury. And lastly, wearing parts must be manufactured of a hardness whose life expectancy would gladden the heart of the Lord of Ten Thousand Years far, far into the future. Yet since no comparable timepiece had ever been built, they had been forced to consider unheard-of experiences and occasionally even pursue a false lead. For even though the Timeless Clock was already running as outlined in the plans, its creators must also make provisions for a future so remote that only an immortal was entitled to see it.

Now though—this was the purpose of the envoy's visit—it was enough. Now it had to be enough. No further signals came from the Emperor, and Cox's companions wondered over meals and at their lathes if everything they recalled had actually occurred: the Almighty One's visits, the many tokens of his benevolence, his appearance one winter's morning, accompanied only by a woman, when he might even have pushed open the front door of a workshop with his own hands . . . An Emperor using his own hands!

Had that really happened? Or had jealous, bitter and hate-filled court dignitaries played a dirty trick on them, leading them to believe that they were in the presence of the Lord of Ten Thousand Years, the Otherworldly One, the Unattainable One, when it had in fact been only an actor or an official in disguise who had spoken to them and asked them questions?

An actor? What an absurd idea. No one would dare, said Kiang; no one in the whole world under Chinese rule would ever dare to imitate the Son of Heaven, not even in a soliloquy, hidden away alone somewhere, not even alone and far out at sea or alone and far out in the wilderness . . . No, no one would consider even *playing* such a role. What had happened, had happened. Now, though . . . now it was definitely not an actor but the Emperor himself who demanded that a promise be kept. He had stretched his patience beyond time and seasons and even halted the summer, indeed the very course of time. Now, though, the signs indicated that even this summer, with its autumn colours, its freezing frost and its blizzards would end.

A train of fifty-two elephants had arrived from Yúnnán and was to be loaded with the consignments for the withdrawal from this suspended time. In the most secretive circles around the Emperor, it was clear that those advisers who wished to dissociate the completion of the monster in the Pavilion of the Four Bridges from the length of the court's stay and imprisonment in Jehol had carried the day.

The English magicians should stay behind in Mongolia while the Emperor went on his way, untroubled by delivery dates! Let the damned clock either be taken with them by elephant, unfinished, or rot in Jehol or finally get started—it should and would not disrupt the life of the court any longer. And as to the elephants: had the generals not procured for the Emperor a new and mighty toy never previously seen on the battlefields he decreed? The march to Běijīng would prove whether these giants could be effortlessly incorporated into the imperial ranks, as their mahouts had promised, adding a new, awe-inspiring, earth-pounding, invincible phenomenon to the Lord of the Horizons' army.

The court would therefore return to Běijīng on the backs of these elephants and of thousands of horses and draught animals, borne in litters and by an endless caravan of carriages, covered wagons and carts, and reinstate the rights of the Forbidden City which had lain dormant for so long, far too long. Time must, and time would, take its course.

Perpetuum mobile: without ever breathing a word of it to anyone, Cox began to wonder during this period if he would really be prepared, if it came to it, to jeopardize a return to England and his own life and those of his companions to realize a centuries-old yearning, to realize *his* dreams! Could he, must he hazard death for a piece that, of all the things he had ever accomplished, was worthy of being called his life's work?

The days had lengthened. Only a few scattered islands of snow lay in the parks, and through the thin veils of mist rising from the riverbanks came the incessant, shrill cries of kingfishers protesting at renewed competition from dippers when, after a sleepless night, Cox presented to his companions the saving idea that freed him from his dilemma regarding the price of his dreams.

It was the simplest solution to a problem neither Merlin nor Lockwood had ever regarded as a threat, and yet they liked their master's suggestion:

A: A rock-crystal knob to open the octagonal column.

B: A cut lead-crystal plug to block or release the stream of mercury.

C: A linear shaft made of gold-plated osmium.

D: A threaded spindle made of hot galvanized Damascus steel.

E: A platinum shaft collar.

These five complementary components, bedded in a silk-lined snakewood casket, said Cox, should be presented to the Emperor along with a set of calligraphic instructions written by Kiang and an announcement that the great work was finished.

The clock could only be set in motion by inserting these five key parts into their proper positions. No one but the Ruler of the World, now a clockmaker himself, now an engineer himself, could be considered to have completed the work. And the three mechanics from England who had assisted him would be allowed to return home unmolested and in peace.

Go home? asked Merlin. Is there nothing more for us to do here?

What else is there for us to do after a work like this? said Cox.

A sundial, said Lockwood. An hourglass. Or a water clock?

For the first time in their stay at the imperial court, the English guests had burst out laughing, sparked by Merlin's chuckle. A water clock! Why not make a steam clock that cooks the perfect boiled egg while we're at it?

Kiang didn't understand what was funny about this conversation and so he did not smile. Cox had asked him that morning to verify a rumour that the elephant caravan had brought to Jehol: a ship belonging to the Dutch East India Company had been towed into Qínhuángdǎo harbour after being caught in a typhoon, and was to be sheathed with lead and undergo repairs there before putting to sea again, with its cargo of porcelain, tea and silk, bound for Rotterdam.

A ship!

The *Sirius*, with which they had sailed to this empire an eternity ago, was still cruising unknown seas and might be prevented by unknown storms and woodworms from bringing three clockmakers home. Also: Qínhuángdǎo was easier to reach than Hángzhōu.

Orion, said Kiang, interrupting their laughter, the ship was the *Orion* and visiting Qínhuángdǎo for the third time. The captain spoke Mandarin and was considered a friend of the country.

What about us? said Merlin. Are we not friends of the country?

But Kiang would not smile at this question either. No, anyone who cast a spell on the Emperor with a pointless game and attempted to bewitch him with a column of toxic mercury was no friend of this country.

Master Alister Cox and his companions would never witness how Qiánlóng reacted to that precious snakewood casket that was brought to him from the Pavilion of the Four Bridges less than four weeks later, along with a mediocre piece of calligraphy that featured five paragraphs detailing how these parts were to be lifted from their silk bed and where they were to be applied so that the Timeless Clock might begin to operate and become a monument to the Emperor's life.

Nobody but the Lord of Time, the sealed instructions said, might set this timepiece in motion. For the life, for which this machine should keep time until the stars expired, was not that of a mortal man but of a god.

Even the bitterest schemers were placated when they learnt circuitously a few days after this parcel had been delivered that His Sublime Majesty was pleased with the glass column and intended to have the English guests escorted to a Dutch wreck that was to be sheathed with lead and fitted with new masts in the docks at Qínhuángdǎo before setting sail for the West. Dead or alive, all that mattered was that these accursed shamans vanished from the Middle Empire. There would surely be enough other opportunities to wipe both their work and all trace of their existence from the face of the Earth.

And so, one bright spring morning, three Englishmen set out from the city towards the South China Sea on the backs of magnificent horses and protected by six armed horsemen (who knew nothing of the diamonds, sewn into silk sashes, with which the travellers had been remunerated by a treasurer barely able to conceal his fury).

Cox had left the construction drawings for his clock and all the tools in locked chests, together with a rice-paper record of the remains of the precious building materials, and he had also advised his companions to travel light. More than a pound of sparkling rose-cut diamonds for each of them represented more than enough funds to pave their paths far into the future.

As he allowed his horse to trot through the snowless, blooming countryside, Cox occasionally whispered to himself some of the words or sentences with which Faye would welcome him. Faye would speak. She would say his name and call to him—yes, *call* to him—how much she loved him. The clock with the mercury heart had brought speech back to her from the other end of the world to Shoe Lane, every stroke of the escapement, every revolution of a cog wheel sent a word back to her room, where the wind flicked the now-open curtains.

Joseph Kiang, who was to accompany the Emperor's guests one last time on their long journey to the docks of Qínhuángdǎo, occasionally fell back so that he didn't have to listen to the master's crazed monologue. Alister Cox spoke of love. He giggled. He laughed.

Jehol had long since vanished behind ranges of gentle hills with a flock of white clouds scudding over them. The city was in the throes of departure. Despite the approach of summer, the court was gearing up for its return to the true heart of the empire, as if time had reversed its direction and was now streaming back, like a river afraid of dissolving and emptying into the sea, towards an auspicious fountainhead.

On the fourth day after the departure of the English guests, a stormy day dedicated to the Jade Emperor, Yù Huáng, the Lord of All the Gods, the Pavilion of the Four Bridges was encircled by a three-line cordon of guardsmen, a forest of spears, glittering needles jutting towards the clouds, ready to repel the very heavens.

The Lord of Ten Thousand Years wished to be alone inside the pavilion with the mysterious thing, toy or monster that the English magicians had brought into the world from the universe. Broad stripes of morning sunshine fell through the windows, setting the octagonal column ablaze, as if it were composed not of metal, glass and mercury but of pure light.

Qiánlóng had moved Master Alister Cox's chair closer to the dazzling thing and opened the snakewood casket containing the five key parts, and was now studying the delicate objects that would set this timepiece in motion. He caught sight of his reflection in the polished black-granite plinth into which a poem he would write at some early morning hour was to be engraved and filled with platinum. But maybe . . . but maybe this Tibetan stone would be better left uninscribed, black, gleaming, empty; a simple reminder of everything that had ever been possible. And was still possible.

Nor did Qiánlóng need the translator's clumsy calligraphy—five instructions for mastering the machine—any longer. In the hours before sunrise, the paper had burnt in a jade dish after he had read it again and again. He would preserve every one of the five steps as an unspoken secret for as long as he could think and remember.

But if he were now to set in motion this piece that struck on and on and on, would that not make the course of time undeniable—a range of measurements to be read by the living and the as-yet-unborn of distant ages—and irrevocable? And would a Lord of Ten Thousand Years still be capable of regulating time to obey his will alone—or would he be pulled along by its current like any of his many nameless subjects?

When the Emperor lifted from its silk bed the lead-crystal plug, with which, according to the last of the five instructions, he could make the river of mercury flow between the clock's cylinders or bring it to a halt, he suddenly felt as if another reminder of the English master had gripped him: a cold draught blowing from the empty lathes.

And so Qiánlóng, the Lord of the Horizons, the Invincible One, shivered, paused and gently replaced the glass plug in its silken hollow.

Lastly

It is worth mentioning, just to be on the safe side, that the name of the real-life clockmaker and automaton-builder whose fantastic works can be seen not only in palatial European museums but also in the pavilions of the Forbidden City in Běijīng, where they beat the time that drives my story, was James Cox and not, as in this novel, Alister Cox.

James Cox never went to China. He did not build any clocks based on the ideas of a Chinese Emperor, nor did he have a wife by the name of Faye nor a daughter called Abigail.

James Cox was neither friends with his historical companion and partner Joseph Merlin, nor did he ever travel with him. The only one of the clocks I describe which they did in fact build together was the one based on the principles of atmospheric perpetual motion—a piece that came closer than any other to fulfilling the unrealizable mechanical dream of a *perpetuum mobile.* Every other clock model in this story is my invention.

Like their descendants to whom I have lent voices, the people who served as models for my characters loved, suffered and feared or mourned for their loved ones. But I could only guess or invent, never affirm, what they felt and what they thought, what they desired and what they might have feared.

Cox and Merlin's patron, the real-life Chinese emperor, who was born in 1711, died in 1799 and bore the era name Qiánlóng ('Heavenly Eminence'), was called Àixīnjuéló Hónglì at birth and revered as Prince Bǎo until his accession to the throne.

Qiánlóng was the fourth emperor of the Qīng dynasty and the only ruler of China to relinquish his throne voluntarily after many decades in power. He had forty-one wives and over three thousand concubines, yet the surviving records mention none called Ān. Qiánlóng collected an abundance of artworks and clocks but he never spoke to an English clockmaker.

Present-day clockmakers and automaton-builders might object that mechanical constructions such as the ones I describe could never have been designed and built in the time I have allotted to them, even by four gifted craftsmen funded by an emperor. That is true.

But the figures in this novel, including Alister Cox, his beloved, mute wife Faye and his daughter Abigail, his companions Jacob Merlin, Aram Lockwood and the unfortunate Balder Bradshaw, yes even the translator Joseph Kiang (who is named after one of my Chinese friends in Vienna), the girlish concubine

Ān and Qiánlóng, the all-powerful Emperor of China and the Lord of Ten Thousand Years, are not characters of our time.

I would like to thank my friends Roy Fox, Joseph Kiang, Manfred Wakolbinger and Zhang Ye: Roy for his research in London on the life of James Cox; Joseph for his guided tour of the Pavilion of Clocks in the Forbidden City; Manfred for his questions that helped me to come up with a good ending; and Ye for accompanying me into the Yellow Mountains of Huáng Shán. It was on the journey into those mountains that a conversation began that eventually resulted in the invention of a country. That country too shares a name with reality: China.

Vienna, January 2016